Beyond The Old Gatehouse

or

Journeys into Fenland

Beyond The Old Gatehouse

or

Journeys into Fenland

STANLEY SCOTT

ISBN: 978-1-78324-266-5

Published by Wordzworth
www.wordzworth.com

This book is dedicated to
John, Owen, Peter, Tom and Jackie,
who as boys, accompanied me on many happy
excursions into the West Fen of Ely.
Thank you for your friendship.

Having completed my first book 'The Old Gatehouse', this sequel takes the Barnes family into fenland, where the 'jewel in the crown' is a cathedral not unlike that here in Ely! Whilst the characters are fictitious, many of the happenings are based on my experiences as a fenland boy, and on later incidents during my working life.

I hope you will get as much pleasure in reading this as I have had in writing it.

Stanley Scott

WITCHFORD, ELY.
AUGUST 2022.

CHAPTER 1

It was late summer and the days were beginning to get shorter. Michael and Lucy had just returned home from sailing on the lake.

'That was lovely!' remarked Lucy. 'I do enjoy being on the water and picnicking on the island. We are so fortunate!'

'I expect it will be the last time before the baby is born,' said Michael.

'Yes,' sighed Lucy, 'it will!'

Just then, Mrs Craddock came into the room to say his lordship had been on the telephone and would Mr

Michael contact him when convenient. Michael immediately went into the study and contacted his father.

'Did you want to speak to me, Father?'

'Yes, Michael. I had Inspector Jakes here this morning, and among other topics of conversation, he mentioned he had been asked to keep a look out for two prisoners who had escaped from a working party. One of these was our old 'friend' Felix! I thought I had better tell you so you can be on your guard in case he tries anything. I've warned William to be careful, so make sure you and Lucy keep vigilant until this man is captured. I have to go to London tomorrow and will be away for a few days – it's an awful nuisance just now before Lucy has the baby!'

'But it isn't due for another week yet, Father!' replied Michael.

Returning to Lucy, Michael told her about the escaped prisoners and his father's reluctance to go up to town just before the baby was due.

'I think your father is more anxious about the baby than we are!' said Lucy. 'It's probably better if he's away, it will help to keep his mind on other things. I can sense the tension is building up with some of the staff too!'

Suddenly, there was the sound of breaking glass.

'Whatever was that?' exclaimed Michael.

'I'll go and see,' sighed Lucy, 'it came from the kitchen!'

Lucy found Mrs Judd on her hands and knees, picking up pieces of broken glass.

'Oh, I'm ever so sorry, Miss Lucy! It just slipped out of my hand. I don't know what came over me!'

'That's all right, Mrs Judd. I think most of us are on edge at the moment. Just clear the mess up and we will say no more about it, but be careful you don't cut yourself!'

'Thank you, Miss Lucy.'

The next day, Lord Barnes caught the train to London, taking care to leave details of his whereabouts should the baby arrive early.

Michael said to Lucy, 'I have to go to see Nigel at the farm this morning, but I hope to be back before lunch, and then this afternoon I must visit the Manor to see Mrs Brookes to make sure everything is ready there.'

'You needn't worry about Mrs Brookes, Michael. You won't find her unprepared, she will have made sure everything is to hand already.'

During the next few days, Michael kept near the house, ready to take Lucy up to the Manor when the need arose.

'I notice your father has been working close by in the gardens!' remarked Michael.

'Yes, I know!' smiled Lucy. 'I think he wants to be near when the time comes. He's like your father – is he coming back this evening?'

'Yes, he is,' said Michael. 'I know he can't wait to get home. Do you think we had better go to the Manor soon so we'll be ready when the time comes, Lucy?'

'All right, perhaps that would be wise. Well, let's have an early night in our own bed and go up to the Manor tomorrow.'

But just as Michael was about to go upstairs the telephone rang. Backtracking to the study, he picked up the receiver.

'Is that you, Michael? I won't be back this evening after all. Someone took a shot at me just as I was about to get into the train tonight, but I'm quite all right so don't worry! I shall be returning tomorrow morning.'

'Good gracious, Father! Do take care. Where are you staying tonight?'

'At Clapham Police Station, so I'm quite safe! I'll tell you all about it tomorrow. Goodnight Michael – and don't worry!'

'Goodnight, Father!'

Joining Lucy upstairs, he told her what had happened.

'You're sure your father is all right, Michael?'

'Yes, Lucy. He told me not to worry. He's unhurt and quite safe, and hopes to be home tomorrow when he will tell us all about it.'

But the following morning, just after seven o' clock, Lucy awoke and gasped, 'Michael, Michael, it's started!' giving him a dig in the ribs. Michael jumped out of bed and ran downstairs to contact Mrs Brookes, nearly knocking into Agnes, who was bringing the early morning cups of tea. On hearing the commotion, Mrs Craddock hurried upstairs to assist Lucy in getting ready to go up to the Manor.

The resourceful Mrs Brookes had everything under control when Michael and Lucy arrived. 'The midwife and nurse are on their way!' she reassured them.

Getting Lucy settled in her room, she said, 'We must let your mother and father know. Mr Michael, will you do that whilst I stay with Lucy until the nurse arrives?'

Mrs Brookes had already warned the kitchen staff to have hot water available when needed upstairs, and William, who had just finished his breakfast, asked if there was anything he could do to help. On being told everything was ready, and not wanting to get in anyone's way, he went into the drawing room to wait for Michael's return.

It was not long before Lucy's mother arrived, and after a brief visit upstairs to her daughter, when she was reassured by the nurse and midwife that everything was going according to plan, she joined Mrs Brookes in her room for a welcome cup of tea.

Meanwhile, Lucy's father looked in at the kitchen to see if all was well, and was offered similar refreshment by Mrs Plum, along with the most recent update!

Back in Mrs Brookes' room, the ladies were on their second cup of tea. Mrs Fanshaw said, 'There's nothing we can do now until the baby is born. I do hope Lucy doesn't keep us waiting too long, you can never be sure with a first child! When is his lordship coming back, Mrs Brookes?'

'This morning. Mr Parry will collect him from the station at eleven o'clock. It was a good thing he had to go to town this week, it gave him something else to think about! Now, will you excuse me for a minute, Mrs Fanshaw? I must see if Maud has taken the tea up to Miss Lucy's room.'

It wasn't long before Mr Parry arrived with his lordship. Mrs Brookes hurried to meet him in the hall and enquired if his lordship was all right after the happenings of the night before.

'Yes, Mrs Brookes, I'm quite all right, thank you. What's going on here?'

'Miss Lucy has started to have her baby, my lord, but don't worry – everything is under control.'

Going straight upstairs, he tapped gently on the bedroom door, and enquired how things were going. Being assured everything was proceeding nicely, he made his way back downstairs to join Mrs Fanshaw and Mrs Brookes.

It was the middle of the afternoon when hot water was called for and there was a lot of to-ing and fro-ing to the kitchen before the faint cries of a baby were heard from upstairs.

Michael, William and Lord Barnes, who had been hovering around in the hall, not really knowing what to do with themselves, quickly made their way upstairs and it wasn't long before the nurse opened the door and invited them in. Michael went straight over to Lucy to see if she was all right. Being told mother and baby were fine, and that he was now the father of a baby boy, Michael bent over and gave his wife a loving kiss. Looking at the tiny child asleep in his mother's arms, he turned round joyfully to his father and brother and said, 'Come and see my son! This is a wonderful day, -I'm so relieved it's all over!'

Lord Barnes was the first to congratulate them both, exclaiming, 'You don't know how happy I am – I now have a grandson! We will have to celebrate properly as soon as you are well enough to join us, Lucy, but in the meantime, we must let you rest.' Turning to Michael and William he continued, 'When we go downstairs you must join me in wetting the baby's head!'

William, who had been looking on in wonder at his nephew all this time, turned to Michael and shook him by the hand saying, 'Congratulations to you both! We have a new little Barnes in our family!'

Michael said, 'It's about time you were thinking of getting married, William!'

'I haven't found the right person yet!' smiled William.

'Well, I shouldn't wait too long!'

'I'll let you know when I've found somebody, Michael!' laughed William.

It was then that the nurse intervened.

'If you don't mind, my lord, I think Miss Lucy should be left to rest quietly.'

'Certainly,' replied Lord Barnes, 'we will leave. Well done, Lucy!'

Giving Lucy one more kiss, Michael made to follow his father and brother. On reaching the door, he couldn't resist turning once more to take a loving look at his wife and baby son.

CHAPTER 2

Lord Barnes wasted no time in making his way to Mrs Brookes' room to impart the good news: 'Mrs Fanshaw, you are now the grandmother of a fine baby boy and all is well. Lucy is resting, but the Nurse will be down to take you to see them both presently.'

'Please excuse me, my lord, I had better let them know in the kitchen and then phone Mrs Craddock,' said Mrs Brookes.

'Please don't worry,' said Lord Barnes, excitedly, 'I'll let them know!' Hurrying down to the kitchen, he found his friend, George Fanshaw, talking to Mrs Plum.

'Is everything all right, my lord?'

'Yes, George! All is very well!' beamed his lordship. 'We are grandfathers to a bonny baby boy, and I'm happy to report that mother and child are doing nicely!'

'Oh, I'm glad that's all over, my lord! Now I can rest, knowing that my daughter is safe.'

'Yes, George, there's nothing to worry about. Please come and wet the baby's head with us all in the study!'

'Thank you, my lord.'

Once the excitement over the new arrival had begun to settle, and Lucy's parents had made their way upstairs to meet the new arrival, Michael said to Lord Barnes, 'Father, tell us what happened in London last night.'

'Well,' said his lordship, 'just as I was about to board the train, somebody fired a shot close by me. I didn't feel anything but people started rushing about and running for shelter. Before I knew what was happening, a man pushed me into one of the carriages and said, 'Keep your head down!' Then after a while, 'It's all right now, we can get out.' Stepping down on to the platform, I saw policemen everywhere. One came up to me and asked if I was all right. It hadn't really occurred to me until that point that I had been the intended target! Then I was escorted into a police car and driven to the police station for my safety, until they found out who had fired the shot. It was already quite late, so I spent the night there until this morning, when they took me to catch my train – and here I am!'

Then Mrs Brookes interrupted the conversation, saying that the Police Inspector had arrived and would like to have a word with his lordship.

'Ask him to come in, Mrs Brookes,' and then turning to Michael and William he said, 'Would you like to join me in hearing what the Inspector has to say?'

'Good afternoon, my lord. I thought you would like to know who fired the shot last night – it was your old manservant, Felix. He is being held in custody pending being sent back to prison. By the way, my lord, he said he only wanted to frighten you, the shot he fired was a blank. I also thought you would like to know who pushed you into the carriage: it was a police officer who had been detailed to keep an eye on you while you were in London since Felix was at large.'

'Well, Inspector, I can't thank you and your boys enough for looking after me.'

After a few days had passed, Lord Barnes asked Lucy and Michael whether they would like to stay on a little longer at the Manor. He thought this would give Lucy more time to regain her strength. They accepted his offer gratefully, much to the delight of the staff, who were enjoying having Lucy and Michael about the house – to say nothing of Lord Barnes, who never missed out on holding his grandson whenever he got the chance!

A week later, Lucy said to Michael, 'I think it's time we returned home. Your father has said we can have the nurse stay to help us as long as we need her. He really has been kind through all this.'

'Yes, I know he has,' agreed Michael, 'he will miss us when we've gone. Still there is one thing he will be pleased about…'

'What's that?' asked Lucy.

'He will get a good night's sleep again! There were several nights when our son just wouldn't stop crying, and being in the next room, my father was kept awake. Although he didn't say anything, I knew there were a few mornings when he would have liked to have stayed in bed a bit longer to recover!'

'I feel a lot stronger now, and we have got into a good routine with baby's feeds, so we must go and thank your father for all his kindness in having us here. I will ask Mrs Brookes to thank the staff too and we must let Mrs Craddock know we will be home in the morning.'

They made their way to the study door. Giving it a few taps, they heard Lord Barnes say, 'Come in!'

Holding hands as they entered the room, Lucy said, 'Michael and I have been talking and we think it's time we returned home, my lord. We are both so grateful to you for letting us be here for the birth of our son, and for looking after us so well. I feel much stronger now and it will be such a help to have the nurse with us at the Old Gatehouse for a little while longer. If we leave tomorrow morning, it will give Mrs Craddock time to get everything ready for our return.'

'I shall miss having you here, to say nothing of my lovely grandson – in spite of him keeping me awake on more than a few occasions, though that's a small price to pay for a first grandchild! Have you thought of a name yet?'

'Yes, my lord,' replied Lucy, with a smile, 'Michael and I would like him to be christened Anthony Cedric Albert Barnes.'

For a moment Lord Barnes stood silent, then he said, 'You have no idea how much that means to me.' Clearing his throat, he added, 'Perhaps when you are home, you would think about when the Christening might be, because I have a few friends I'd like to invite!'

Michael said, 'We will let you know, Father, and give you plenty of time to send out your invitations!'

'Well, the Great Hall is here at your disposal whenever you want it.'

'Thank you, Father, that will be perfect!'

At dinner that evening, Michael said, 'How many friends were you thinking of inviting to the Christening, Father?'

'Well,' said Lord Barnes, 'probably about twenty. There were a few who couldn't get to your wedding, so perhaps we could send them an invitation to the Christening and hope that they can come this time.'

'We have several people to invite on Lucy's side of the family as well,' said Michael. 'Now, what about you, William? Do you have anyone you would like to invite?'

'I can't think of anyone at the moment,' replied William, 'but if I do, I'll let you know. By the way, Father, were you thinking of asking Lord Fortesque from Craig Lodge?'

'Well, yes, my boy, I was, along with his wife and daughter. They couldn't come to the wedding because Lady Fortesque was unwell, so I hope they can make it this time. I'll let you have my list, Michael, and then we can begin sending the invitations out.'

CHAPTER 3

The next morning, Lucy and Michael said their goodbyes to Lord Barnes and the Caiston Manor staff, and returned home to the Old Gatehouse. Mrs Craddock was pleased to see them back, and eager to have a look at the new arrival.

'Have you thought of a name for him yet, Miss Lucy?'

'Yes, Mrs Craddock, we will call him Anthony Cedric Albert Barnes. 'Cedric' after his lordship!'

'Oh, that's a lovely name!' exclaimed Mrs Craddock. 'By the way, the pram arrived during the week. It's in the lobby, Miss Lucy.'

'Thank you, Mrs Craddock. Now, just to confirm – the nurse will be here for some time yet, so is Agnes ready to move into another room upstairs while the nurse is here?'

'I have already seen to it, Miss Lucy, and I've put the letters which have come for you on your desk, Mr Michael.'

'Thank you, Mrs Craddock. It's nice to be home, I'd better go and see to things now,' said Michael.

'Nurse has already taken our son upstairs, but I'd like to make sure all is well, so I'll just go up and see. Thank you, Mrs Craddock.'

After they had finished lunch, Lucy said, 'We really must give some thought to the Christening. I was wondering about four weeks from now? That should give enough time for the invitations to be sent out and the replies received. Your father is anxious to show his grandson off to all his friends, Michael, and I know my father is looking forward to it as well! Providing it's all right with his lordship, we ought to see the vicar to arrange a suitable time.'

'Yes, let's do that,' agreed Michael.

'Will you telephone your father to arrange to talk things over in the morning then?'

'Yes, I'll go and call him now.'

'Miss Lucy!'

'Yes, Mrs Craddock?'

'I know you have only just returned home, but have you decided when the Christening is going to be? The reason I ask is that Cook was wondering if she could have two days off to visit her sister who is very ill, and she didn't want to be away when she would be needed in the kitchen for the celebrations.'

'Oh, that's all right, Mrs Craddock. Tell Mrs Judd it will probably be in about four weeks' time, and that we hope she finds her sister a little better when she sees her.'

'Thank you, Miss Lucy.'

At that moment, Michael returned and said, 'My father will look forward to seeing us both tomorrow morning at ten o'clock.'

So the next day, Michael and Lucy went up to the Manor to see Lord Barnes.

'And how is my grandson this morning?' he enquired.

'Oh, he's on fine form!' replied Michael. 'He kept us awake half the night, but we're beginning to get used to that now!'

Lord Barnes smiled, 'I must say there were a few nights when I missed out on some sleep -as you know! Now, when you have made out your list for the Christening, please let me have it and I will see that the invitations are sent out from here.'

'Thank you, my lord,' said Lucy, 'that will be such a help. Michael and I will give you our list tomorrow but we particularly want to talk to you about getting in touch with the vicar.'

'Yes, that's most important. Ask him if he would come here to the Manor, so we can arrange a date and time,' replied Lord Barnes.

'Very good, Father,' said Michael. 'We will see to it!' and during the next few days, all the arrangements were put in place.

'Now all we need is for the sun to shine!' thought Mrs Brookes, as she walked down to the kitchen to see Cook.

She found Florence and Maud already there, enjoying a mid-morning cup of tea with Mrs Plum.

'Florence, while I think of it, did Mr Jolly ever fix that door on the linen cupboard?'

'Yes, Mrs Brookes, he did – and what a mess he made doing it! I should know, I had to clear it up.'

'Well, I'm glad it's fixed because we will be having all the guest-rooms full for the Christening,' said Mrs Brookes.

'I hope that Colonel and Mrs Parks won't be staying -I still remember the night-cap incident from last time!' exclaimed Maud.

'I don't know who will be staying,' went on Mrs Brookes. 'His lordship will give me the names when the replies to the invitations are in.'

As the weeks went by, everything was ready for the guests to arrive, but it was only two days before the Christening when Lord Barnes finally handed Mrs Brookes the list of those who would be coming.

'You will see, Mrs Brookes, that Lord Fortesque, his wife and daughter will be here for about a week. Will you put them in the room next to mine, and their daughter in a room on the other side of theirs?'

'Very good,' said Mrs Brookes.

'Lord Fortesque is an old friend and we will have a lot to talk about. William will be here to help me welcome the guests as they arrive.'

The next morning, after breakfast, Lord Barnes said, 'William, you will be on hand to greet Lord Fortesque, his wife and daughter, won't you? I have to go down to see Michael to give him the quarterly returns on the Estate and I might not be back in time. They will be here about mid-morning and I don't want Lord Fortesque to arrive with nobody from the family here to welcome him.'

'Very good, Father, I will be here.'

After Lord Barnes had left to see Michael, William said to Mrs Brookes, 'I will be in the drawing room if anyone should call. The Fortesques are expected here later this morning.'

'Yes, your father has told me,' replied Mrs Brookes.

About an hour later, the front door bell rang. William got up from his chair and went into the hall only to find Mrs Brookes already on her way to answer it, and on opening the door, there stood Lord Fortesque and family.

'Come in, my lord, we are expecting you.'

William went forward to shake hands and to introduce himself. Lord Fortesque said, 'This is my wife, and this is my daughter, Caroline.'

Shaking her warmly by the hand, William said, 'Welcome to Caiston Manor! Would you all like to go to your rooms to freshen up after your journey? Mrs Brookes will show you the way. Then perhaps you might like to join me in the drawing room for some refreshment? My father will be back shortly.'

It was Caroline who came down first.

'Shall we go into the drawing room, Caroline?' said William, who had been waiting around in the hall. 'Have you come far?'

'We left home about two and a half hours ago,' replied Caroline. 'We had a good journey. Daddy told me we might be staying on for a few days after the Christening, which will make a nice change.'

'Do you ride, Caroline?'

'Whenever I get the opportunity. My Uncle Bertram has a farm in the fen country, and when I go to stay, I go riding with his daughter, Mary. They have several horses on the farm, as well as all the other animals. I like Uncle Bertram, he's a bit of a joker – he makes me laugh!'

William said, 'Would you like to go riding while you are here? I'm sure we could find you a horse and then I could show you around the Estate.'

'That would be lovely,' replied Caroline.

CHAPTER 4

'William said I could go riding with him about the Estate while we are here,' said Caroline, as Lord and Lady Fortesque came into the room. 'That will be nice,' replied her mother.

Looking at William, Lord Fortesque said, with a grin on his face, 'Mind you take good care of her – we don't want any little accidents!'

'Oh, I will make sure everything is all right – you have no need to be worried.' William knew full well what Lord Fortesque was referring to: no jiggery-pokery in the hay-loft! 'My father should soon be back. He had to go down to see Michael about something. Caroline was telling me about her Uncle Bertram.'

'Yes,' replied Lord Fortesque. 'She often goes to see my brother at his farm in the Fens. It's very different from the countryside around here – you can see for miles and miles it's so flat – but the land is some of the best in the country. The soil is jet black in places and produces some fine crops, but I don't think I'd like to live there, in spite of the wonderful sunsets. I have another brother who has taken a very different path in life. -Aha! I think I can hear your father, William.'

Just then, Lord Barnes came into the room, and shaking his old friend by the hand, said, 'I'm sorry I wasn't here when you arrived, Charles.'

'Oh, that's all right, Cedric! William has been looking after us.'

'Did Mrs Brookes show you to your rooms?'

'Yes, Cedric. We have been looked after very well, and William and Caroline seem to be getting on splendidly. William is going to take Caroline riding.'

'Yes, I'm sure we can find a good horse for your daughter,' replied Lord Barnes, 'there are some very pretty rides around here, especially now the trees are beginning to turn to their Autumn colours – I will have to take both of you round the Estate while you are here.'

'We'd like that, Cedric, wouldn't we, Emily?'

'Yes, dear, that would be lovely.'

After lunch, Lord Fortesque's wife said, 'If you will both excuse me, I think I will have a lie-down for a little while before the rest of the house guests begin to arrive. I know you both will have a lot to talk about!'

'Yes,' replied Lord Barnes. 'We have! William, why don't you show Caroline around?'

'All right, Father, I was just going to ask Caroline the very same thing! Do you think you had better take your coat, Caroline? I know it's a sunny day, but it soon gets cold when the sun goes down.'

Making their way to the study, Lord Fortesque said, 'You know, Cedric, I think Caroline has taken a shine to your son. She doesn't usually take to young men as readily as this, but she appears to be quite at home in William's company.'

'I think it's a good thing, Charles,' replied Lord Barnes, 'otherwise your daughter would be at a loose end, so to speak. She will be quite safe with him, he knows how to behave himself! They will be good company for each other. Since Lucy and Michael had the baby, William has missed out on seeing his brother. They get on well together, but Michael spends more time now with his son.'

'That's understandable,' replied Lord Fortesque.

As William and Caroline left the Manor, he said 'I hope you are not too tired from your journey to walk to the farm? I thought we could have a word with Nigel, the farm manager, to see about a horse for you to ride, but first, I will take you round by the lake to show you the island. There's not much there, only trees and bushes, but in the springtime it's covered in primroses.'

'Are there any wild orchids there?' asked Caroline.

'I don't know,' replied William. 'Are you sure this is not making you too tired, Caroline?'

'No,' she said, 'this is such a lovely part of the country. That must be the wood your father was talking about?'

'Yes,' said William, 'in the Spring, the hedgerows are all out in blossom and in the Autumn, the trees are a picture to look at.'

'Are there nightingales in the woods, William?'

'I don't really know, Caroline, but we could always go and listen one evening if you would like to?'

'Yes, I would,' replied Caroline.

They walked along in silence for a little while, as if each was thinking of something to say; then they spoke at the same time which made them both laugh!

'You first, Caroline,' said William.

'I was just going to say, I don't know many young men. It's true one or two have wanted to go out with me, but I just haven't been interested in them. I'm glad I've come today though – I do enjoy your company, William. You remind me a bit of my Uncle Bertram, only you are younger! I'm sure if you met him, you'd like him too. He is so full of fun and makes everyone laugh!'

'Perhaps I will be able to visit him one day. By what you've said, I feel I know him already,' remarked William.

Soon, they came to the farm buildings, and looking around, they found Nigel in one of the barns.

'Hello, Nigel! This is Lord Fortesque's daughter, Caroline. Miss Caroline and her parents are staying with us at the Manor for a few days and I was wondering if we have a horse available for her to ride while she is here?'

'Yes, I'm sure we can find one. When would you be wanting it?'

'Oh, it will have to be on Monday now,' replied William. 'It's the Christening tomorrow.'

'Leave it with me,' said Nigel. 'I'll see both horses are brought up to the Manor on Monday morning.'

'Thank you, Nigel.'

Making their way back to the Manor, William said, 'I must have a word with my father now. Would you mind if I left you for a little while, Caroline?'

'Of course not. I will see if my mother is awake – she ought to be by now!'

'You might find her in the drawing room, Caroline.'

'I'll go and see.'

William made his way to the study, where he found his father and Lord Fortesque in serious conversation.

'Is everything all right, father?'

'No, I'm afraid it's not,' replied Lord Barnes. 'We have just been told this country will soon be at war with Germany.'

'Do we know what is going to happen?' enquired William.

'Not at the moment,' replied Lord Barnes, 'I expect they will be conscripting men for the armed forces now. Thinking about tomorrow, William, will you be about to welcome some of the guests who will be arriving for the Christening?'

'All right, Father. I will be here.'

The next morning, after breakfast was over, Lord Barnes and his guests made their way to the church, soon to be joined by Michael and Lucy, with baby Anthony.

The little church was full of people, all eager to witness the christening of Anthony Cedric Albert Barnes, who didn't take kindly to the experience, and showed his objection by crying all the way through the service!

When it was over, the family and guests made their way back to the Manor for some refreshment, preceded by a short speech from Lord Barnes, in which he thanked everyone for coming, and wished all those travelling, a safe journey home.

Now we take a leap in time and join our story sometime after Anthony's fifth birthday. Michael and William are safely home from the war where Michael had been serving in the Royal Navy, and William – for the last two years of the conflict – in the Army...

CHAPTER 5

Michael and William were at the Manor discussing Estate business with his lordship, when Lord Barnes announced, 'I've been thinking about having a war memorial erected somewhere on the Estate. It will be in the form of a cross and at the base of it will be the names of those Estate workers who lost their lives in the recent conflict – including Cousin Robert. In addition I should like the following words inscribed on the arms of the cross:

'FORGET NOT THOSE WHO DID NOT RETURN'
and then the whole thing surrounded by a low enclosure

so relatives may come and pay their respects and lay flowers if they wish. Now, what are your thoughts?'

'I think that would be a very good idea,' said Michael.

'So do I,' echoed William, 'and I am also concerned about their families – we can't turn them out of their houses to make way for the replacement workers.'

'No,' replied Lord Barnes. 'That has been on my mind as well. We must leave them be for the time being, but will you both give some thought as to what we should eventually do? We must start to recruit men to fill the vacancies because we will soon be losing the Germans who are working on the farms – and I must say, I don't know what we would have done without their help. I must have a word with Mr Parry about that too.'

Leaving the study, Michael said to William, 'It's not going to be easy getting replacements without being able to provide living accommodation for their families. I think we have got to put a lot of thought into this, William. Consider it today and let's meet tomorrow morning so we can sort something out before we next see Father.'

The following morning, William duly arrived to talk to Michael.

'Come in!' said Mrs Craddock. 'Do you want to see Mister Michael? If so, you will find him in the study.'

'Yes, thank you, Mrs Craddock.'

The two brothers spent the rest of the morning discussing how they could resolve their present labour shortage without turning the families out of their homes.

'If only we could house those families affected somewhere else on the Estate, leaving the workers' cottages with their large gardens, for the new workforce.'

'Well,' said Michael, 'I was thinking something like that, but only if the Estate could afford it. We would need a row of six two-bedroomed cottages with small gardens for the families concerned, that would free up the present accommodation for the new workers and their families – but this would take a while to do. Meanwhile, we could begin to engage replacements with a promise of accommodation when it becomes available, and perhaps pay those workers a little extra for their inconvenience?'

'That would seem to be the best way forward,' said William.

So that afternoon, they went to see Lord Barnes, who welcomed their suggestions. Then he said, 'We have another problem: I had Mr Parry here this morning, who said one of the Germans wants to stay here working on the farm. He doesn't want to go back to Germany, but Mr Parry thinks there is more in this than self-preservation. He has been seen talking to Mrs Druly – who lives next door to the Fanshaws – not just once, but several times. I don't know what the legal implications are regarding an ex-prisoner of war becoming involved with a British subject, but I must make some enquiries.

Regarding the suggestions you have both made, I will contact the architect to see what is involved in putting this in hand. If we can build a row of six cottages – each with a small garden in front – on the edge of the Estate next to the village, the tenants would have easy access to all the village facilities. That would leave the present cottages with their large gardens available for the new workforce. Until the new homes are ready we must do what we can to keep everything on schedule. Fortunately, we've had two years with really good crops, which means we might just be able to put this plan into operation.'

Smiling at his two sons, he continued, 'Now the warmer weather is on it's way, I think it would be a nice gesture to hold a party here for the Estate workers' children. It would be a way of thanking the families for their loyalty during the recent hardship.'

When Michael arrived home, he told Lucy all about his father's idea of holding a children's party at the Manor, finishing by saying, 'We will need some help in organising this. Perhaps we could invite one or two friends as helpers? I know William will be pleased to join in.'

'Has he got a girlfriend?' asked Lucy. 'If so, he could bring her.'

'I could ask him,' said Michael. 'Although he keeps very quiet about his love life, I know he disappears now and then! He used to be sweet on Caroline Fortesque. It would be just like him to spring it on us one day that he's going to get married!'

At that moment, William walked in.

'We were just talking about you!' said Lucy.

'Nothing untoward, I hope?'

'No, we were trying to decide who might help with the children's party and wondered if you had anyone you would like to invite to help?'

'No,' replied William.

'A little bird told me you were seeing someone,' remarked Michael.

'Well, your little bird has got it wrong!' laughed William.

'Don't play the innocent with us, William,' teased Lucy. 'We know you used to like Caroline Fortesque at one time – do you still see her?'

At that, William coloured up. 'Well, I do occasionally bump into her.'

'By what I have been told,' went on Michael, 'you should have a good many bruises by now! Come on, William, own up!' he said, with a laugh.

'Well,' said William, 'it seems I will have to tell you: I have been seeing Caroline.'

'So shall we ask her to the party then?' said Lucy, 'it would be nice to see her again.'

'That's settled then,' said Michael, '-we'll ask her anyway!'

Feeling a little bit awkward, William said, 'Could I have a word with you, Michael?' Then, going into the study he said, 'It was Caroline I wanted to see you about this morning. I've actually asked her to marry me and I'm waiting for her reply.'

'Well, that's marvellous news!' exclaimed Michael. 'You are a dark horse!'

'But please don't say anything yet until I know,' begged William. 'I have been asked to stay with the Fortesques on the weekend, so I shall know something then. You can tell Lucy, but don't say anything to Father yet – I want to tell him myself!'

After the two brothers had finished discussing matters relating to the Estate, William said, 'I think I should be off now.' So saying goodbye, William returned to the Manor, leaving Michael to tell Lucy the news, though not saying anything to anyone else.

CHAPTER 6

On the Wednesday morning, William went to see his father. Tapping on the study door he heard, 'Come in, -oh, it's you, William! Is anything wrong?'

'No, Father, but could I have a word?'

'Yes, fire away!' said Lord Barnes.

'I've been invited by Lord Fortesque to stay at Craig Lodge for the weekend. I have been seeing his daughter, Caroline, a few times. In fact, I have asked her to marry me and I expect her to give me an answer on the weekend.'

'Well, bless my soul!' exclaimed Lord Barnes. 'How long has this been going on, William?'

'On and off ever since Anthony's Christening, just over five years ago,' replied William.

'Well, I never!' said Lord Barnes, shaking his son by the hand. 'Caroline would make you a good wife. Her father and I go back a long way and I have many happy memories of time spent in his company. I hope all goes well for you this weekend. Give my regards to Lord Fortesque when you see him.'

'I will,' replied William.

Friday morning came and William set off on his travels to Craig Lodge. He was asked in by the butler who said he would let Miss Caroline know of his arrival, but just at that moment Caroline appeared and said, 'That's all right, Franks. I will look after him.'

Going right up to William, Caroline whispered in his ear, 'Yes!'

Immediately, William threw his arms around her and they both kissed, lost in the moment until Franks coughed, 'Huhum… would there be anything else Miss Caroline?'

Turning to face him, she said, 'No, that's all, thank you.'

'You have no idea what it's been like this last week since I asked you to marry me,' said William. 'I've been longing for this moment! Now I know it's all right, I feel on top of the world!'

'We had better go and find Mummy and tell her our news, I know she'll be delighted!'

'And then we must go and find your father,' said William, with some trepidation.

Arm in arm, they went in search of Lady Fortesque and found her sitting reading in the drawing room.

'Mummy, we have something to tell you: William has asked me to marry him and I have said 'yes'!'

Getting up from her chair, Lady Fortesque said, 'Congratulations my dears, I hope you will be very happy together!' Then she gave them both a kiss and said to William, 'Welcome to our family! My husband and your father are close friends and I'm sure he has more than an inkling of what has been going on!'

At that moment, Lord Fortesque came into the room. Seeing three happy faces, he said, 'Hello, William! It's nice to see you again…'

'Well, Daddy, William has asked me to marry him and I have said 'yes'.'

'Gracious me!' said Lord Fortesque. 'I must say I've been expecting this, and I couldn't be happier for you both.'

'Thank you, my lord. It had been my intention to ask you first, but things have moved faster today than I'd anticipated!'

'Now we'll have plenty to talk about – have you thought when you would like the wedding to be?'

'We haven't had time to discuss a date yet,' replied Caroline, 'but I hope it won't be too long.'

'By the way, my lord, my father asked me to give you his kind regards,' beamed William.

'Likewise, when you return home, young man.' After giving the bell rope a tug, he said, 'Well, Emily, this calls for a little celebration! -Ah! Franks! Will you bring us four glasses and a bottle of champagne, we have an occasion to celebrate!'

Once Franks was on his way, Lord Fortesque continued, 'We must let the rest of the family know our good news.'

Caroline said, 'Won't Uncle Bertram be surprised? – and also Uncle Harold! I hope we can be married in the cathedral. We'll have to go and see Uncle Harold to find out if it's possible.'

'Will your Uncle be able to tell us? Is he something to do with the cathedral then?'

'Yes,' replied Caroline. 'He's one of the canons there.'

'Well, that should help!' smiled William.

'I will contact my brother,' said Lord Fortesque, 'and find out for you if you would like me to?'

'Yes, please, Daddy. That would be kind.'

William and Caroline spent the rest of that weekend making plans for their wedding.

'We will have to find somewhere to live,' observed William. 'Since I help my father and Michael to run our Estate, it would be advantageous if we lived somewhere not too far away from there.'

'Well, I'm sure we can find something, dear.'

On returning home after his romantic weekend at Craig Lodge, William went to see his brother to tell him the news and to ask him if he would be his best man at the wedding.

'Of course, I will!' replied Michael. 'You know, you are a man of surprises, William! I had no idea until last week that you were even courting. When is the wedding going to be?'

'We haven't got a date yet. Caroline and I don't want to have a long engagement but we have to find somewhere to live first.'

'Yes, that might be a problem,' remarked Michael. 'I hope you will still be able to help in running the Estate. Well, Lucy and I both wish you all the very best and if there is anything you want to know, or anything I can help you with, you have only to ask.'

'Thank you Michael, you're very kind.'

Going back to the Manor, William went to see his father to convey Lord Fortesque's warmest wishes and to say that he and Caroline would be getting married in the not-too-distant future.

'Well, that is good news!' remarked Lord Barnes. 'Charles Fortesque and I have been friends for a long time, and to think that my son will be marrying his only daughter is simply wonderful! I shall have to contact Charles and tell him how happy I am that our two families will be joined together when you are both married.

Now, you must tell me if there is anything I can help you with – you only have to ask.'

'Thank you, Father. Everyone is being helpful. We have several things to sort out; most particularly, whether we can be married at the cathedral in Beeley and then to solve the problem of where we are going to live.'

'I think between Charles and myself we should be able to find you something suitable,' remarked Lord Barnes.

'I have been asked to stay again this weekend,' said William. 'We have to start making out the guest list for the wedding.'

'I know,' said Lord Barnes, 'there is a lot to do, so, as I've said, if I can be of any help, just ask.'

'You are kind, Father, thank you very much.'

'By the way, William, I must have a word with you and Michael concerning this German worker business. I had Mr Parry here yesterday to see me and apparently the situation is more serious than we first thought. I understand from him that Matt Schulz wants to marry Mrs Druly. This opens up all sorts of problems – for one, will the rest of our tenants want to be living next door to a German?'

'I see what you mean, Father,' said William. 'Shall we have a word with Michael to see what his reactions are?'

'I think we had better,' replied Lord Barnes.

CHAPTER 7

When William went to visit Caroline the following weekend, Lord Fortesque said he had been in touch with his brother, Harold, and as far as Harold knew, it should be possible for the wedding to be held in the cathedral. He continued, '-there is one thing which must be observed: because William is not resident in the cathedral parish, he must either obtain a special licence or spend at least three nights there in order to comply with parish requirements. My brother has said he has plenty of room in his house and could help with that: in fact, he can accommodate four or five people for the wedding itself, so that won't be a problem.'

'Well, that's good,' remarked William.

'I hoped Uncle Harold would say you could stay at his house,' remarked Caroline, 'it's very old and right beside the cathedral. It was built in the thirteen hundreds on the site of the old infirmary. He has a housekeeper to look after him – her name is Mrs Good. She has a daughter, but she works away and only comes home occasionally.'

At this point Lord Fortesque said, 'I had better let you get on with the wedding arrangements, there's always a lot to be done. You know where to find me if you want me!'

By the time the weekend was over, most of the arrangements had been made except the date and time of the wedding, which needed to be confirmed with Uncle Harold before the invitations could be sent out.

Caroline said, 'William dear, could you stay for a few days longer when you come next weekend, then we could go over to see Uncle Bertram and family?'

'Yes, I expect that could be arranged. I don't think I shall be needed for anything urgent at home – in any case, Michael will be there to see to it!'

'Well, that's settled,' said Caroline, with a smile.

When William arrived home, he asked his father if he could be spared a little longer the following weekend, as Caroline wanted him to meet her Uncle Bertram and family.

'Yes, of course,' replied Lord Barnes. 'Michael will be around, so there will be the two of us here.'

'Thank you, Father. By the way, Lord Fortesque's brother has offered to accommodate us all in the lead up to the wedding. The house is in the cathedral precinct, and I may need to stay there for three nights before the wedding anyway, since I don't live in the cathedral parish. It will be very convenient as I understand it's quite an awkward journey to Beeley from here. I had better let Michael and Lucy know that they can stay there too.'

Leaving his father, William made his way down to the Old Gatehouse to tell Michael and Lucy that Uncle Harold was happy to accommodate them all.

'At present I can't tell you exactly when the wedding will be,' said William. 'I may have to be resident in Beeley for a few nights first in order to be married in the cathedral. It's a complicated journey to Beeley, so it's a good thing we all have somewhere to stay.'

William spent the next few days getting his case ready for the weekend, helped by Mrs Brookes, who made sure he had everything he needed with him for his extended visit.

Finally, Friday came and William set off to see Caroline. When he arrived, Caroline said, 'I thought we would go to Uncle Bertram's tomorrow. You will like it, I'm sure, although it's very different countryside from where you live.'

So, on the morrow, Caroline and William set off for Uncle Bertram's. As they travelled along, William was amazed how flat the countryside was becoming and all too soon they arrived at Wentley Village station. They were met by Arnold, Uncle Bertram's eldest son, who took them to the farmhouse where Aunt Annie and Cousin Mary were waiting to greet them.

'Let me introduce you to William,' said Caroline.

After they had shaken hands, Mary said, 'When's the wedding going to be?'

Caroline answered, 'We're waiting to hear back from Uncle Harold on that – we hope to hear very soon.'

Taking them into the house, Mary said, 'Mum has been getting the attic room ready for William, and as usual, you, Caroline, can sleep in the single bed in my room. We will have a jolly time tonight when all the family are home!'

After William had deposited his case upstairs and rejoined the ladies, he said, 'Darling, I've got a lovely view of the countryside from my attic window – I think I'm going to like it here!'

'I hope so,' replied Caroline. 'I have so many happy memories of this place. Ever since I was a little girl, coming here has always been special – Uncle Bertram's family have made me welcome every time.'

'That's nice!' smiled William.

Following Mary into the living room, Caroline said, 'When will Uncle Bertram be home?'

'He'll be back in time for supper, especially as he knows you are going to be here! He's looking forward to meeting William – as are all the family.'

'I am deeply honoured!' remarked William, with a laugh. Getting up and turning round to cover his embarrassment, he said, 'What a lovely room this is!' Then going over to the window, he looked out.

'Is that a swing I can see, over by the tree?'

'Yes,' replied Mary. 'Although once I fell off it and skinned my knees, Caroline and I have had a good many happy times on that swing. Caroline, you must take William and let him try it out!'

CHAPTER 8

There was a delicious aroma of cooking coming from the kitchen. 'Oh, I do feel hungry!' said William. 'Something smells good!'

'Yes,' replied Caroline, 'you wait till we sit down to eat!'

Just then, Peter, the youngest son, came into the room.

'Hello, Caroline! Is this the William I've been hearing so much about?'

'Yes, indeed,' replied Caroline.

Shaking William by the hand, Peter said, jokingly, 'There's a ginger-headed boy down the road who's sweet on Caroline, so don't let her out of your sight while you're here, William!'

'Now that's enough of that, Peter,' said Mary. 'He's pulling your leg, William! He's a joker, just like his father – always out for a bit of fun.'

'You can say that again!' said Mary's mother, coming into the room. 'I must get the table set, Father will be home soon.'

'Can we give you a hand?' enquired Caroline.

'We both will,' said Mary.

'I'll have a chat with William while you are all busy setting the table,' remarked Peter. 'What's involved in running an estate, William?'

'Well, we have an Estates Manager who oversees everything, and he reports to us each day. My father is getting on, and leaves the running about to my brother Michael and myself. If we require new stock, one of us usually goes with the farm manager to buy them. Do you work on the farm, Peter?' asked William.

'Yes, I help my father, together with Harry Wood – who drives the tractor, and old George Halfsharp..'

'Who?' enquired William, starting to laugh.

'Old George Halfsharp has been with us a long time. He's very good with looking after the cows, especially when they're calving.'

William, still chuckling to himself, and seeing Caroline come back to put some plates on the table, said, 'Caroline, dear, do you know Old George Halfsharp?'

'Yes, I've seen him around when I have stayed here,' replied Caroline. 'Why?'

'Well, Peter has been telling me about him – his name made me laugh!'

'Oh,' said Caroline.

'Peter, we've met your older brother, Arnold,' said William, changing the subject.

'Yes,' replied Peter. 'Arnold works for the Electricity Supply Company as an electrician. After collecting you from the station, he had one or two jobs to do. He should be back soon.'

'I'll look forward to seeing him again.'

Mary said, 'Caroline, I think we've just about got everything ready now – why don't you get up the table with William and Peter? I can help Mother bring in the food when it's ready.'

'All right, Mary, I will.'

Just as she was about to sit down with William, Uncle Bertram appeared. 'Where's that lovely niece of mine?' he said.

Caroline went over to give him a kiss, 'This is William, Uncle.'

'You are a very lucky man, William. If I had been thirty years younger I would have given you a run for your money. Take good care of her or you will have me to answer to!'

'-And me!' said a voice.

'Oh!' exclaimed Caroline. 'It's Arnold! How was your afternoon?'

'All the better for seeing you, Caroline.'

'Go on with you! How's work?'

'Busy at the moment. When is the wedding going to be?'

'We're waiting to hear from Uncle Harold. I hope it won't be too long, but William has got to stay at Uncle Harold's for a few days before the wedding so we can be married in the cathedral.'

'Oh, I wouldn't stay there if I were you, William – it's a strange place!'

'Why?' asked Caroline.

Just then, Mary's mother came into the room and asked everyone to take their places at the table. This they did with alacrity, and soon were tucking into some wholesome farmhouse fare, enjoyed by all.

It was an hour and a half later before they made their way to the parlour, where, of course, conversation was centred around the forthcoming wedding.

Then Uncle Bertram began to tell William all about the fens, and how, at one time – a long while ago – they were covered with trees, later to become submerged as the fens turned into swamps and were covered in reeds. 'Even today,' he said, ' we occasionally find one of those trees when we're ploughing. We call them 'bog oaks'. They're black in colour and very hard to cut with a saw. We let them dry out and then cut them up for firewood. One of these logs will last most of an evening and throw out a great deal of heat. In a dry spell, we often have what's known as a 'fen blow' – this usually happens when there's a strong westerly wind, which whips the soil into clouds of dust and off the fields into the dykes.

Now, William, you and your family must join us in the summer when we have our Harvest Supper. We hold it in one of our fields, weather permitting, and Annie puts on a real feast. After that we play games – do you know the one where somebody goes off and has to try to find their way back without getting caught by the rest of us? We always give him a head start before we chase after him. It sounds a bit silly, but I can assure you it's great fun – especially if somebody falls in when we jump the dykes!'

After a glass of homemade wine, which had a rather soporific effect on them all, they nodded off one by one until Caroline came to with a start, and giving William a shake said, 'William, dear, I think it's time for bed!'

'It's been a lovely evening... Is it always like this?' enquired William.

'Mostly,' replied Caroline. 'Sometimes Aunt Annie sits down at the piano and we have a singsong.'

'I bet that's fun!'

'Yes, it is!'

When Caroline and William got up from the sofa, most of the family followed suit – all except Uncle Bertram, who was still fast asleep and snoring loudly.

Quietly, they made their way upstairs to bed. William, tiptoed up to his attic room, and like the rest of the household was soon fast asleep, and would have over-slept the next morning if it hadn't been for the swallows squabbling outside his bedroom window!

CHAPTER 9

After breakfast, Caroline and William walked down to the farm. Caroline wanted to show William the horse she usually rode when she went to stay at Uncle Bertram's.

'Has your Uncle got many horses?'

'There are three to choose from when we want to ride about the fields. My uncle has built some jumps – not very high ones – just big enough to make it interesting!'

As she was speaking, they heard someone say, 'Is that you, Miss Caroline?'

Turning round, Caroline exclaimed, 'George! I was just going to show Mister William the horse I ride when I come to stay.'

'You will find him in the usual stable, Miss Caroline.'

'William and I are going to be married, George.'

'Well, I hope you both will be very happy together,' replied George, 'but I wish you had brought some better weather with you, Miss Caroline! It looks like it's going to rain again – I think we had better take shelter in the barn. I hope it won't be much, but you never know.'

Sitting down on some bales of straw, Caroline said, 'You look after the cows, don't you, George?'

'Yes, Miss, that's my job, though I do other things on the farm as well.'

'You must like working with animals, George, you've been here a long time.'

'I like all animals, Miss, except rats and foxes which do harm, although my brother had a pet fox once.'

'How did he manage to get that?' enquired William, who up till then had kept silent.

'Well,' said George, 'my brother and some of his farming friends went on a shoot one Sunday morning in the fens because the foxes were becoming a nuisance, going after the chickens in some of the farms around here. Their dogs found a burrow near a hedge, and when my brother investigated, he discovered seven little fox cubs. Now, some folk would have destroyed them, but they were very weak and obviously orphans, so, my brother, being soft-hearted, brought them home with him and fed them with warm milk from a baby's bottle. He put them in a cardboard box, lined with a flannelette sheet, to keep them snug.'

'That was kind of your brother,' remarked Caroline.

'What happened to them?' asked William.

'Well,' said George, 'they all died except one.'

'Oh, how was that?' exclaimed Caroline.

'Well,' said George, 'it was no fault of my brother's. A friend of the family said he knew someone who wanted a fox cub as a pet, and my brother knew that when they grew up he could not have seven foxes running about the place, so he let him have two.

After a week had gone by, the family friend returned with the two foxes, saying that when he went to see how they were doing, he found the gardener putting them into a pail of water because they would not eat the meat he had given them. My brother's friend said, 'Give them to me, and I will take them back to be with the other fox cubs.' Unfortunately, they'd caught a chill which they passed on to the others, and they all died except for one, which my brother called Willy.'

'What happened to him?' enquired William.

'Well,' said George, 'he grew up so he could run about the house. My mother put a rug over the settee which stood on four legs. This rug had tassels which hung down over the front of the settee, and when anyone came into the room, Willy would run under the settee to hide and all you could see of him was his nose, peeping out through the tassels!

As he grew bigger, my brother made a kennel for him outside and put him in a collar – just like a dog. This was fastened to a long chain which allowed him to run about outside. My brother's two dogs used to play with him, and sometimes he would break free from his collar and run off into the orchard next door, chased by the two dogs, and when he had had enough, he would return back to his kennel!' George went on, 'It's a funny thing, you wouldn't think a fox would like chocolate.'

'No,' replied William, 'you wouldn't.'

'Well,' said George, 'my brother used to meet up with some of his farming friends in the evening at the local pub for a game of darts, and when it was time for him to go home – about half a mile away – he often used to whistle while he walked along. At the top of the road, was a gate with slot machines on it. One of these machines dispensed chocolate covered wafers, and my brother knew he would have someone waiting for him when he got home! As soon as he got near, Willy would hear my brother whistling, and start screeching and making all sorts of noises, but when my brother gave him the chocolate wafer, which he gobbled up, he quite happily settled himself down for the night. On one or two occasions, my brother forgot the chocolate. Willy just would not settle, and my brother had to go back to the slot machine before he got any peace.'

'What happened to Willy?'

'My brother was asked by a farmer friend if he could have him on his farm, and as it wasn't right to keep a fox chained up for the rest of his life, my brother knew Willy would have more freedom there so he let him go.'

William said, 'He must have been quite tame then.'

'Yes,' replied George. 'One evening, before he gave the fox away, my brother took Willy with him, on a lead, when he went to post a letter up in the town. Going past the entrance of an ironmonger's shop, which had an iron gate across the entrance, someone made a noise which frightened Willy and he shot through the railings into the doorway, and no amount of coaxing would get him out. It wasn't long before there was a crowd, all eager to see the fox, which didn't help my brother, who was having real difficulty trying to entice him out. Finally, my brother had to lean over the railings and lift him out. That was the one and only time my brother took Willy for a walk!'

Caroline, who up till now had been quiet, said, 'What an extraordinary story, George!'

'Yes, I know,' replied George, 'but it's quite true. My brother did miss him for quite a time after that – even though he did it for the best.'

CHAPTER 10

'I think it has stopped raining now, Miss Caroline.'
'Yes, George, we can carry on with our walk now. Thank you for telling us that story. I do hope Willy was happy in his new surroundings. Come on, William!'

As they walked along, William said, 'Doesn't the air smell fresh after the rain?' Then looking at Caroline he added, 'You were very quiet while George was telling us about that fox…'

'I know. I found it quite moving to think a wild animal would behave like that – and what about it liking chocolate?'

'You never can tell,' remarked William. 'Fancy old George being able to remember it in such detail.'

'Look, William! There's the field with the jumps where we used to go and ride.'

'Perhaps Uncle Bertram could find me a horse while we are here, then we could go riding together.'

'We must ask him when we get back,' replied Caroline, 'but I expect Mary will want to come too.'

'Oh, can't we go, just the two of us? I don't seem to have had any time alone with you since we have been here!'

'Well, we can't very well not ask her, it is her father's farm.'

When they returned to the house, Mary said, 'Caroline, I've got some magazines which you are welcome to take with you when you go back.'

'That'll be nice!' replied Caroline. 'I like looking through magazines, especially if they have the latest fashions in them.'

'They're upstairs in my room,' said Mary, 'so I will give them to you later on this evening.'

'Thank you,' replied Caroline.

'Mary!' called out her mother, 'Would you start to set the table for lunch?'

'Right, Mother!'

When she left the room, William lost no time in kissing Caroline.

'Someone will come in, dear!'

'Let them! I've been waiting all the morning to do this!' Then giving her another kiss, he said, 'I've got some catching up to do!'

'Oh, William!' She flung her arms around him and they remained like that until they heard Mary cough as she stood in the doorway.

That evening, at supper, the conversation got round once more to the wedding and Uncle Harold.

'He has been at Beeley about seven or eight years. Before that he was vicar of a little place called Salthouse,' said Uncle Bertram. 'As Arnold says, he lives in a strange house. I've only been there once. I think it was built shortly after the cathedral. They are all very old houses around there. Arnold can tell you more about it as he did some work there several years ago.'

William was just about to ask Arnold, when Peter butted in and said, 'Can we have a singsong after supper?'

'Oh, yes, please!' said Caroline.

'You'll have to ask Mother,' said Uncle Bertram, glancing at his wife.

'Very well – as soon as we've cleared the table!'

'You will love this, William. I hope you'll join in – it's good fun, you'll see!'

William wasn't so sure, though Caroline must enjoy it so why shouldn't he?

To his surprise, the singsong came to an end all too

soon with a rousing chorus of 'Widdecombe Fair', after which they all trooped off happily to bed.

Next morning, Caroline said, 'Dearest William, Mary and I are going for a little ride after breakfast and when I get back, there will still be plenty of time for us to go riding together too.'

'Oh, all right,' said William, though by the tone of his voice he was not most pleased.

This was the start of things going wrong between them and by lunchtime they were scarcely speaking to each other. Caroline spent the rest of that day with Mary. As for William, he felt thoroughly miserable and was glad when it was time for bed.

After a sleepless night, William went down to breakfast feeling wretched at how things had turned out. He and Caroline had been getting on so well together – what had happened to bring about this rift between them?

While they were having breakfast, Mary's mother, sensing how unhappy both William and Caroline were, said, 'Can't both of you stay another day, Caroline?'

'No, I'm afraid not, Auntie. William has got to get back to help out on his father's Estate.'

'Oh, that's a shame,' replied Mary's mother.

So when they had finished breakfast, William and Caroline said their farewells and set off on the return journey to Craig Lodge. They hardly spoke a word to each other all the way back and when they arrived, William said bluntly, 'I must be on my way home now.'

Caroline, feeling utterly dejected at what had happened between them, went up to her room, threw herself down on her bed and wept.

On his arrival home, William was met by Mrs Brookes who asked if he had had a nice time. William didn't say a word but went straight upstairs, feeling as though the bottom had dropped out of his world.

CHAPTER 11

When Lord Barnes heard that William had returned, he went to find his son to hear about his stay at the farmhouse. Seeing Mrs Brookes, he asked if she had seen him.

'I think he went up to his room, my lord.'

'Well, when he emerges, will you tell him I would like to have a word?'

William didn't appear until dinner that evening and sensing something was wrong between his son and Caroline, Lord Barnes tried to find out what the trouble was, but William was too upset to want to talk about what had happened. Instead he asked how things were on the Estate.

Knowing it was no use pursuing his enquiry further, Lord Barnes changed the subject, saying, 'I think next time you see Lucy, she may have something to tell you.'

William mumbled, 'Oh, that will be nice,' and then was silent for the rest of the meal.

When dinner was over, Lord Barnes went to his study and, picking up the telephone, spoke to his old friend, Charles Fortesque, to find out if he knew what the trouble was between William and Caroline.

'All I can tell you at the moment is that Caroline is very upset and is staying in her room, crying, and no amount of pleading will get her out.'

'Well, I don't know!' said Lord Barnes. 'It must have been some disagreement! If only we knew what it was, between us we might manage to do something about it.'

'I quite agree,' said Lord Fortesque.

'Shall we leave them alone tonight and see how things are in the morning, then I will have a word with William if you can talk to Caroline, and we might get them speaking again? I'll give you a call before lunch, Charles.'

'Very well, Cedric – till tomorrow!'

At breakfast, the next morning, Lord Barnes said to William, 'You know, true love never runs smoothly, but when you have time to think, it usually wins through in the end. You and Caroline are just right for each other and because of some silly disagreement, you have both made each other thoroughly miserable. Now, my boy, after breakfast, you will pick up that telephone and call Caroline to say how sorry you are – even if it wasn't your fault. That usually does the trick, if you know what I mean?'

Seeing his father meant business, William said reluctantly, 'All right, Father, I will.'

At Craig Lodge, Lord and Lady Fortesque were having a more difficult time in trying to win Caroline round. At last, she relented and said she would give William a call. Just as she was about to do so, the telephone rang.

'Is that you, William?'

'Yes,' replied William. 'I have missed you terribly. I do love you and I'm sorry for making you so unhappy. Can we meet up soon to put things right?'

'Oh, yes, my darling,' said Caroline.

(This was when Lord Barnes interrupted the conversation by saying to William, 'Go straight away!')

'I can come this morning to see you, dear.'

'Come as soon as you can!' replied Caroline, 'I will be waiting for you!'

Replacing the receiver, William turned to his father and said, 'Thank you for making me see sense. I do love Caroline, and this has been such a silly misunderstanding between us. I will see it never happens again.'

When William arrived at Craig Lodge, he and Caroline spent the afternoon making up for lost time, only appearing hand in hand when it was time for dinner with Caroline's parents.

'Caroline, I have heard from Uncle Harold who has confirmed that you may be married in the cathedral.'

'Oh, that is good news – thank you for telling us, Father.'

Lord Fortesque continued, 'He has confirmed the day and time – it's in four weeks, so we must get the invitations sent out right away. There's no time to lose! I have been in touch with your father this afternoon, William, and he will be sending a list of guests from your side of the family, although most people have already been told to expect an invitation as soon as a date and time were fixed. Arrangements have been made for you, William, to stay at Uncle Harold's on the Wednesday, Thursday and Friday nights before the wedding. Your brother and family can stay on the Thursday and Friday too, and since the wedding celebrations are likely to last until midnight, they can't be expected to travel back home then, so Uncle Harold has said they can stay until the Sunday.'

'That's very kind of Uncle Harold, Daddy – isn't it dear?'

'Yes,' replied William, who secretly could not help feeling a bit uneasy about it, remembering what Caroline's cousin, Arnold, had said about Uncle Harold's house – and still wondering why.

There were no more tiffs in the weeks leading up to the wedding. All the invitations had been sent out. William and Caroline had spent considerable time together, checking the invitation list to make sure no one had been missed off.

'Like your father, dear, Daddy knows a lot of important people, so we must get it right. Will you have to go home tomorrow?'

'I'm afraid so,' replied William. 'I've yet to get packed, ready to stay at your Uncle's.'

'I shall miss you,' said Caroline.

'And I, you,' said William, giving her another kiss.

'It won't be too long now,' said Caroline, 'and then we'll be together on our honeymoon.'

'I'm looking forward to that,' replied William.

CHAPTER 12

The next morning, William said his goodbyes, and giving Caroline one last kiss, departed for home. On arrival at Caiston Manor, William went straight to see his father to give him an update on the wedding arrangements. He concluded by saying, 'Mrs Brookes has got everything ready for me, so I shall soon be leaving to catch the train to Beeley.'

Wishing his son a safe journey, Lord Barnes said, 'I will be with you on Friday. I'll see you then.'

Collecting his case, William made his way to the front

of the Manor where Mr Parry was waiting to take him to the station.

Eventually the train arrived at Beeley. William got out and enquired the way to Uncle Harold's house. As he walked up the hill from the station, he remembered what Uncle Bertram had told him about the fens once upon a time being covered with reeds, which made it necessary for the villages and towns to be built on higher ground.

Making his way under the archway, he followed the path round towards the cathedral. Having never seen anything like it, he stopped, admiring the spectacle before him. Then he turned and made his way along Nun's Walk to Cowchester Hall, the home of Uncle Harold.

Ringing the front doorbell, he had only a few moments to wonder what he was going to find inside, when suddenly the door was opened by Mrs Good, the housekeeper.

'You must be William! Come in – we've been expecting you. Canon Fortesque is in the cathedral at the moment, and I have instructions to make you a cup of tea after showing you to your room.'

William followed Mrs Good upstairs. He was able to leave his case and take a few moments to freshen up before returning along the landing, then down the back staircase leading into the kitchen, where Mrs Good was already busying herself at the kitchen table preparing the evening meal.

'Come in,' she said. 'Do sit down, the kettle's nearly boiled. Is this the first time you've been to Beeley?'

'Yes,' replied William. 'Isn't that a magnificent building outside? I don't think I have ever seen anything like it before!'

'We're very proud of it. I know the canon will want to show you inside the cathedral tomorrow.'

'I shall like that,' replied William. 'Have you been here long, Mrs Good?'

'About five years. I arrived here shortly after the canon was appointed. So! You are going to marry Miss Caroline, the canon's niece?'

'Yes,' said William, 'I've known Caroline for several years. You don't know how much I'm looking forward to Saturday!'

'Well, it won't be long now!' smiled Mrs Good.

Then William said, 'I think I ought to go and hang my wedding things up as soon as I've finished my cup of tea – I don't want them to be creased for my big day.'

A few moments later, he put down his empty cup and saucer, saying, 'Thank you for that, it was most welcome!' Then he made his way up the backstairs to his room.

Drawn to the view outside his window, William stood looking at the magnificent building. He opened the window and straightway heard the organ being played at the end of evensong. This went on for about five minutes during which William could not help but think, 'In three days' time, I will be in there, getting married!'

When the music finished, he closed the window and went back downstairs.

It was not long before Canon Fortesque came through the door, and seeing William – who was engaged in conversation with Mrs Good – said, 'I'm Caroline's Uncle Harold, you must be William!'

'Yes, sir,' said William, shaking him by the hand.

Canon Fortesque said, 'Now, why don't you call me Uncle Harold? In a few days you will be part of the family.'

'Thank you, Uncle,' replied William.

'I expect you would like to see inside our beautiful cathedral?'

'Yes, indeed!'

'Well,' said Canon Fortesque, 'I will take you in tomorrow morning after Mattins, about ten o'clock.'

'I will look forward to that!'

'Now, we usually have our evening meal in about an hour's time, does that suit you, William?'

'Yes, that will do nicely!'

Turning to Mrs Good, Canon Fortesque said, 'I will take William into the drawing room until supper time.'

'Very good, Canon Fortesque.'

'If you follow me, William, I will show you the way.'

Going through the front hall, the Canon led him up the main staircase, into the drawing room.

'What a lovely room!' exclaimed William as he settled himself down on one of the couches.

'Have you been to Beeley before, William?'

'No, this is the first time, Uncle.'

'I hope you've managed to find your way around so far. This is a big house and keeps Mrs Good busy all the time.'

'I understand it was built in the thirteen hundreds on the site of the old infirmary.'

'Yes,' replied the canon, continuing, 'I think we have your brother and family coming tomorrow and your father, the day after?'

'That's right,' said William.

'We will have a houseful on Friday!' remarked Canon Fortesque, with a chuckle. 'That will keep Mrs Good out of mischief – although I think she's got someone coming to help her for the next few days! Nonetheless, there will still be a lot to do.'

'It's very kind of you to have us all staying here with you for the wedding.'

'Not at all,' replied Uncle Harold. 'I'm only too pleased to be of help.' Hearing the gong in the hall, he added,

'It's supper time, William. Follow me.'

Both men went down the front stairs and into the dining room. This was another large room and looking around, William commented, 'What an enormous fireplace!'

'Yes!' said Canon Fortesque. 'I think most of the houses around here have large fireplaces…'

Just then, Mrs Good came into the room with the supper tray and very soon, conversation gave way to the serious business of eating!

CHAPTER 13

William enjoyed his meal, and afterwards, he and Canon Fortesque retired to the drawing room for some liquid refreshment until William said, 'I think I will have an early night. It's been a busy day and I have enjoyed every minute of it. Goodnight, Uncle, and thank you for everything.'

He was about to leave the drawing room the same way as he'd come in, when Canon Fortesque said, 'Not that door, William, but this door over here! This will take you on to the landing where your bedroom is.'

'Goodness, this house is quite a puzzle! Thank you once again,' said William. 'Goodnight!'

When William emerged from his room the next morning, the smell of cooking greeted him as he made his way down the back stairs into the kitchen. He found Mrs Good busy at the stove. She called out a friendly, 'Good Morning, young man!'

'Good Morning!' William replied.

'Did you sleep well?'

'Yes, I certainly did, thank you.'

'Breakfast is served in the dining room.'

'Oh,' said William, 'I should have gone the other way!'

'Please don't worry,' said Mrs Good. 'You can go through the front hall and into the dining room that way if you like.'

William crossed the kitchen to the far corner, where he opened a door covered in green felt, behind which was yet another door, leading into the front hall.

'That's strange!' thought William, surprised to find two doors so close together. Then he crossed the hall and went into the dining room.

William sat down at the table, and looked around the room. While he was waiting for his breakfast, his eyes were drawn once more to the huge fireplace. Suddenly, to his surprise, he saw the outline of a figure standing there, then – just as quickly – it was gone! At that moment, Mrs Good entered the room with his breakfast.

'I must have imagined it!' thought William, so didn't say anything to her, deciding to mention it to Uncle Harold when he next saw him.

It was just after ten o'clock before the canon arrived home, and finding William in the drawing room, asked if he was ready to see inside the cathedral. William had been looking forward to this enormously, so together, they walked across and entered the cathedral by the South Door. Moving into the Octagon, they sat for a few minutes whilst Uncle Harold gave William a brief history of the cathedral.

'There used to be a monastery on this site, founded by St Etheldreda – you can see her shrine before the High Altar. The building of the cathedral began in the eleventh century, but in thirteen twenty-two, the central tower collapsed. So great was the noise that the monks nearby thought there had been an earthquake. It took twenty years to rebuild and this is what you can see above us now. The Octagon and Lantern are world famous. -Now, how is your head for heights?'

'Pretty good, I think, Uncle! Why?'

'I'll take you up into the roof space above us so you can look down to where we are sitting now. You will also be able to see some of the huge timbers used in its construction. Follow me!'

Going into the North transept, Uncle Harold opened a door, behind which were steps leading up to the roof space above. After pointing out the large beams around them, Uncle Harold opened one of the Angel Doors so William could look down – ninety feet below! It quite took his breath away, but once he had adjusted to the vastness of the building, he started to picture the day of the wedding, and how he might feel when he first saw Caroline walking up the aisle towards him…

Returning back down the stairs, they entered the Lady Chapel, where Uncle Harold drew William's attention to the statues, which had suffered at the hands of Cromwell's men when they used the Lady Chapel as a place to stable their horses.

Re-entering the cathedral, they walked up the North Choir aisle, stopping to admire the ornate stonework over the entrance to a little chapel at the east end of the cathedral, then moving behind the High Altar and down the South Choir aisle into the Octagon again.

This is when Canon Fortesque remarked, 'I could do with a sit down before I take you down the Nave. My legs are not as young as they used to be!'

After a while, they made their way down the Nave towards the West Door and Uncle Harold pointed out the location of the stairs which led to the top of the West Tower, adding, 'I'm sure I could find someone to take you if you'd like to go up, but it's a little more than I can manage at my time of life! The view of the surrounding countryside is well worth the effort. On a clear day, it's said you can even see the outskirts of Cambridge, which is about fourteen miles away.'

As they strolled back to the South Door, William said, 'What a magnificent building! Thank you for showing me round, Uncle.'

'It's a pleasure, William. I don't know about you, but my legs ache!'

'Yes, even I will be glad to have a sit-down!'

As they left the cathedral, Canon Fortesque looked at his watch and said, 'We have a few minutes before lunch is ready – would you like a glass of sherry, William?'

'Oh, yes, please, Uncle Harold, I would.'

'Where are you and Caroline going for your honeymoon?'

'We're going to Scotland. In fact Caroline and I will be catching the six thirty train from Beeley station after the wedding, and travelling through the night, arriving at our destination about breakfast time the next morning. I expect we'll both be tired after a journey like that! Still, we'll be on our honeymoon and just the two of us – I'm looking forward to that,' smiled William.

'-Ah! That's the gong for lunch,' said Canon Fortesque. 'We mustn't keep Mrs Good waiting!'

CHAPTER 14

After lunch, William made his way to the station to meet Michael and family. As soon as Anthony saw William he shouted out excitedly, 'We saw a lot of swans and geese on the water, there were lots and lots of them, Uncle William!'

'Well I never!' said William, looking up at Lucy, with a broad grin on his face. 'Did you have a good journey?'

'Yes,' replied Michael, 'but the train went very slowly as we came across the washland. They seem to have had more rain than we've had back home. What's it like here?'

'Very nice, Michael. You wait until you see inside the cathedral – it's enormous! Uncle Harold – that's what he wants us to call him, took me up into the Lantern and I was able to look right down into the space below. You can also go up to the top of the tower and see all the countryside around.'

'Oh, I should like that,' said Michael, 'but I don't know about Lucy!'

'No thank you! I'll let you two go up on your own!'

'Can I come too?' asked Anthony.

'No,' replied Lucy, as the cathedral came into view. 'I don't think your little legs would be able to take you all the way up to the top of that tower. Look how high it is!'

As they reached the end of Nun's Walk with the cathedral immediately before them, Michael exclaimed, 'I can see what you mean – what a wonderful building it is! I'm going to like spending time here, William. I'm longing to see inside. Perhaps Uncle Harold will take us tomorrow?'

'Yes, I'm sure he will,' replied William.

'Anthony and I will have a look round if you two want to go up to the top of the tower,' said Lucy. 'I wonder what your father will say when he sees this, Michael?'

Approaching Cowchester Hall, William said, 'I think I had better go in first. We don't want to give Mrs Good a fright -she's the housekeeper.'

Opening the front door, William called out, 'It's all right, Mrs Good, it's only me! I've got my brother and family with me.'

The kitchen door opened, and Mrs Good appeared.

'Pleased to meet you. Come in! You must be tired after your journey – I'll show you where you will be sleeping tonight. Follow me.'

Taking them up the main staircase, she led them through the drawing room on to the landing.

'I've put your son in the little room at the far end. It's got a good view of the cathedral and I've made up a little bed especially for him. You are both in the room next to him with William on the other side.'

After they had refreshed themselves, they joined Mrs Good downstairs for a welcome cup of tea.

It was just after five o'clock when Canon Fortesque returned home from the cathedral. William lost no time in introducing his brother, sister-in-law and young Anthony.

'I expect you are pleased to have two days off school, young man?'

'Oh,' said Lucy, 'Anthony has his own private lessons at home with Mr Frankley. They seem to be getting on well together and it also gives the kitchen staff a bit of peace and quiet!'

'I expect William has told you something about the cathedral,' said the canon.

'Yes, we can't wait to see inside it, Canon Fortesque.'

'Please call me Uncle Harold – after all, when William and Caroline are married we will be part of the same family! I will take you inside after Mattins tomorrow, that will be about ten o'clock.'

'William tells me it's possible to go up to the top of the tower, Uncle.'

'Yes, you will need to go up with a guide, either at eleven o'clock in the morning or three o'clock in the afternoon. It takes a little while – depending on how many stops you take – and on a clear day you can see for miles around, so they tell me!'

'Do you have a very large choir here, Uncle Harold?' enquired Lucy.

'At the moment there are sixteen boys and six lay-clerks, with two supernumerary clerks joining the choir on a Sunday. Most of the boys live locally. Any that come from away have to find accommodation nearby. They have a busy schedule, singing twice a day.'

'What about their schooling?' asked Lucy.

'Oh, they have their own school on the other side of the cathedral. There are about twenty-five to thirty pupils with two masters to teach them, and their lessons are fitted around their rehearsals and services in the cathedral.'

'They certainly have a busy time,' remarked Lucy.

'They certainly do,' agreed Uncle Harold.

Turning to Michael, Lucy said, 'I would like to go to a service tomorrow, will you come with me?'

'Yes, let's all go. We can take Father with us if he gets here in time. What time is the service tomorrow afternoon, Uncle?'

'Four o'clock, and you want to be in your place ten minutes beforehand.'

Looking round, Michael commented, 'This must be quite a large house, Uncle, to be able to accommodate us all for the wedding.'

'Yes,' remarked Canon Fortesque. 'We haven't had a houseful like this for a long time. We had to bring the spare room into operation in order for you all to stay. We haven't ever used that room before, as far as I can remember. Mrs Good will have her hands full this weekend!' He laughed, 'That will keep her on her toes!'

It was then that the gong sounded. 'Ah! It's time for supper,' he continued, 'I hope you're all hungry.'

'I'm famished!' said William.

'So am I,' said Michael.

'It must be our fenland air!' chuckled Canon Fortesque, 'it's bound to give you all an appetite!'

After supper they talked about the wedding and the place where the reception was to be held.

'It's not far from the cathedral, just a stone's throw away. You must have walked past it on your way here,' said Canon Fortesque.

As the evening progressed, Anthony started to show signs of tiredness and Lucy said, 'I think it's time for little people to go to bed.'

Not wanting to miss anything, Anthony said, 'Can't I stay up a bit longer, Mummy?'

'You've had a busy day and if we are to explore the cathedral tomorrow, you will need your rest so you can walk around.'

After a little while, Lucy took Anthony to his room, and getting him safely tucked up in bed, whispered, 'Goodnight and sweet dreams'. Then, tiptoeing out of the room, she went to tell Michael he needed to hurry up in saying 'goodnight' to his son, because he was already half asleep.

CHAPTER 15

'Where is Uncle Harold this morning?' Michael asked as Mrs Good brought in the breakfast.

'Oh, it's his turn to take the early service this week and then he has Mattins at nine o'clock. He's already had something to eat so you needn't wait. I hope you all slept well?'

'Yes, thank you,' replied Lucy. 'I must say we had a very comfortable bed.'

'Yes,' said Mrs Good, 'the canon bought that bed from a shop in Cambridge when he first came here. He entertained the bishop one weekend and the bishop slept in that very bed.'

'Oh!' said Michael, with a laugh, 'we are honoured!' Then turning to Lucy, he said, 'By the way, dear, I mustn't forget to meet Father at the station this morning. He said he would be arriving at eleven twenty, so if you like to take Anthony into the cathedral with Uncle Harold, William and I will meet Father and come on to join you there.'

So, after breakfast, whilst Lucy took Anthony to wash his face and hands before meeting Uncle Harold, Michael said to William, 'It's such a nice morning, shall we have a stroll and explore this part of Beeley before going to the station?'

'That's a good idea,' said William.

Leaving Cowchester Hall, the two brothers set off on their walk, finishing up at the railway station in time to meet their father, who said he was more than glad to arrive after a very tedious journey with the train stopping at every station.

Michael said, 'Never mind, Father, you wait till you see the cathedral! Lucy has taken Anthony inside with Uncle Harold and we will be joining them after dropping your case off at the house. We thought you would like to have a look round before the wedding rehearsal later.'

They found Uncle Harold talking to Lucy and Anthony who, when he saw his grandfather, jumped up and would have run over to meet him if Lucy hadn't told him to walk!

Once pleasantries had been exchanged, Lord Barnes said, 'I could do with a sit-down!' At that, Anthony scrambled on to his grandfather's lap as Uncle Harold proceeded to tell them all a little more about the history of the cathedral, adding that if anyone would care to explore the tower, a guide could take them that afternoon at three o'clock.

'Yes, please, I would!' piped up Anthony.

'I think we agreed that would be too dangerous for you, dear,' said Lucy, 'the steps would be too steep for you to climb.'

Lord Barnes quickly saved the situation by saying, 'You can stay with me and keep me company, Anthony. I can't climb up all those stairs, but one day when you are older and your legs are longer, you can come back with your father and explore and then tell me all about it!'

'Now,' said Uncle Harold, 'are you ready to see round the cathedral?'

'Yes, I think we all are!' said Michael.

Getting up, they followed Canon Fortesque, who took them on a short guided tour.

When they had finished, Canon Fortesque said, 'I must leave you now, there's about another fifteen minutes before lunch so I will see you back at the house.'

Lucy said, 'Anthony will be tired after all this walking.'

'He's not the only one!' said Lord Barnes, with a grin on his face.

After lunch, Lord Barnes said, 'Would you mind if I had a nap? I've done quite a lot of walking since I got off the train this morning!'

'Of course not, Father,' replied Michael. 'Lucy said she would like to see the shops while we're here, so we'll come and collect you about a quarter to four, in time for the afternoon service.'

'That will suit me perfectly,' replied Lord Barnes.

So they left him to have his nap and made their way through the arch to the High Street. As they walked along, Michael said to Lucy, 'I would like to come back to Beeley one day to have a really good look around, and if we could find somewhere to stay, we wouldn't need to bother Uncle Harold.'

'Well,' said Lucy, 'we've just passed a hotel called 'The Bell'! It looked quite nice. We could always try there.'

'That would be a good idea, and we'd be near enough to be able to return Uncle Harold's hospitality, without him having three extra people in his house!'

Half an hour later, Lucy said, 'I think we ought to be getting back to Uncle Harold's if you and William want to go up the tower at three o'clock. Anthony and I can have a little rest and freshen up before we collect your father and go to the service.'

'That's a good idea,' replied Michael. 'It looks as if Anthony could do with a bit of a tidy-up, but I must say he's been a jolly good boy with all this walking.'

Anthony beamed.

About an hour later, Lucy, Anthony and Lord Barnes made their way over to the cathedral for Evensong, sitting down in the Octagon with Michael and William, ready for the service to begin.

At four o'clock precisely, the choir made their way out into the Octagon and up to the choir stalls. The service lasted about three-quarters of an hour, and when it was all over, Michael said, 'I wouldn't have missed that for anything! I thought it was lovely.'

'So did I,' added Lucy.

When the organ had finished playing, they were joined by Uncle Harold, who asked William to confirm that Caroline would be joining them for the wedding rehearsal at a quarter past five.

Once the rehearsal was over, they returned to Cowchester Hall for supper, eventually retiring to the drawing room for a glass of port – with the exception of a very sleepy Anthony, who was given a glass of warm milk!

'I hope that doesn't make him want to get up in the middle of the night!' remarked Michael.

'Oh, he'll be all right,' said Uncle Harold, 'he has the necessary receptacle in his room should he need it!'

'That's a relief!' said Lucy.

'Yes,' chuckled William, 'in more ways than one!'

'As soon as Anthony has finished his milk, I think I'd better get him settled in bed,' said Lucy.

On Lucy's return to the drawing room, Lord Barnes, who had kept unusually quiet, said, 'I should just like to say, sitting as we did this afternoon, listening to the choir singing, with the shafts of sunlight streaming down on us from the windows high up in the south transept, that I have never felt so moved. The singing, the sunlight and above all the peaceful atmosphere in there, has made me realise how lucky we are to have such wonderful buildings as this. May they last forever.'

Nobody spoke for at least two minutes, then Lucy reflected, 'Didn't the flowers by the choir gates look lovely?'

'Yes,' said Uncle Harold. 'You will have seen some of the helpers arranging them earlier this morning. They take a lot of trouble.'

Feeling the effects of a very busy day, Lord Barnes said, 'I don't know about all of you, but I am ready for my bed! As for you, William, I'd like to have a little word with you before you turn in.'

CHAPTER 16

The gong sounded, and one by one they made their way down to the dining room for breakfast. Lord Barnes was the last to arrive saying, 'I had a job to find my way!'

'Yes,' said William. 'The first day I was here, I thought I was going to the dining room, but I ended up in the kitchen where Mrs Good was cooking breakfast!'

Right on cue, Mrs Good came into the room.

'I hope you all slept well?'

'Yes, thank you, Mrs Good.'

'It's another lovely morning – just right for your wedding, William.'

Lord Barnes looked up, rather surprised at William not being called 'Mister William' at the very least.

'Well,' continued Mrs Good, 'I'll leave you all to have your breakfast in peace.'

Breakfast over, Lord Barnes said to William, 'Would you like me to help you get ready for your wedding, William?'

'Thank you, Father – Michael has offered to help me.'

'Well in that case, I'll go and get myself ready, and then put my feet up until it's time to go!'

It had been decided that both brothers would wear their service uniforms, so Lucy dressed Anthony in a sailor suit.

When the time came, William – in Army uniform, and Michael – in his Naval uniform, joined the rest of the family and made their way over to the cathedral, taking their places ready for the service to begin.

William said, 'There are a lot of people here, Michael! I wonder how Caroline is feeling? She said she would be a few minutes late, as is customary, and not to worry! I will be glad when it's all over and we are on our honeymoon. How did you feel on your wedding day, Michael?'

'Like you, William! I was relieved when Lucy and I were on the train and it was all over!'

'Caroline told me that some of her father's friends from the law courts are coming.'

'We'll have to be on our best behaviour then!' smiled Michael. 'I do hope Anthony behaves himself today, sometimes he can be a little outer when he wants to! He's been telling Lucy all sorts of nonsense about seeing things at night in his bedroom.'

'Oh?' said William, 'I've never forgotten what Cousin Arnold said when I told him I'd be staying here – he said, 'I wouldn't stay there, it's a strange house!' but before I could ask him why, I was interrupted by Peter, his younger brother, who suggested a singsong!'

'Well, I shouldn't say anything to Lucy, it will only worry her. Here we go, William, it's time!'

Both brothers stood up as Caroline, on the arm of her father, began her walk up the aisle towards them. When she drew level with William, he whispered in a low voice, 'You look lovely!'

Then both of them turned to face Uncle Harold, who was standing there ready to marry them.

After the vows had been exchanged, William, with Caroline on his arm, together with the two fathers, followed Uncle Harold to sign the register whilst the choir were singing.

A little while later, bride and groom made their way through the Choir Gates to the strains of the Wedding March, emerging from the South Door into the sunshine, where they were soon surrounded by guests and well-wishers who showered them with confetti.

Then followed the photographs, after which the wedding party made their way down to Cherry Tree Lodge for the reception.

Both Lord Barnes and Lord Fortesque wished William and Caroline good health and happiness in their lives together. The customary speeches by groom and best man came next, with William thanking everyone for coming and for the many gifts he and Caroline had received. He also stated that after the honeymoon, he and his wife would be residing at Willow Tree Lodge, on the edge of Lord Fortesque's estate.

When the meal was over, the newly married couple went up to Cowchester Hall to change. Collecting their cases, they returned to the reception to say their farewells before leaving for the station.

William thanked Michael for being his best man, and on saying goodbye to Anthony, was asked where he was going.

'I'm going away on my honeymoon.'

'Can I come?' asked Anthony.

Michael laughed and said, 'I don't think Uncle William and Auntie Caroline would want you with them on their honeymoon!'

'What's a honeymoon, Mummy?'

'It's like going away on holiday, only it's very special,' said Lucy.

'Can we go on a honeymoon then, Mummy?'

'One day when you are grown up and fall in love with a nice young lady, and get married, you will be able to go away on your honeymoon, but for now Anthony, no more questions!' said Lucy, giving him a hug. 'Let's go and wave Uncle William and Auntie Caroline off!'

So the wedding party made their way to the station, where William and Caroline boarded the train to Scotland. As it moved out, there were cheers from the large number of family and friends assembled on the platform, all intent on waving them off until the train disappeared into the distance.

Later on, back at the reception, Lord Barnes and Lord Fortesque were talking together when Hilda Warboys approached them and enquired where William and Caroline were going on their honeymoon.

Hilda Warboys was an old friend of Lord Fortesque, so he promptly introduced her to Lord Barnes, who was interested in what she had to tell him about her travels abroad, especially those in Egypt, when she was out there with her late husband. By the time the evening was over, Lord Barnes had promised to invite Hilda Warboys to stay at Caiston Manor.

'Did you see how that woman latched on to your father, Michael?' remarked Lucy, sometime later.

'Yes, I did, and I wouldn't be surprised if we were to see her again at the Manor!'

'Who's that, Mummy?' asked Anthony.

'Never you mind! It's well past your bedtime young man! Michael, I think I should take Anthony back to Uncle Harold's now. If he's not tired, I certainly am!'

'All right, dear, I'd better stay a while longer to keep an eye on Father before we both return!'

CHAPTER 17

It was midnight before the party broke up. A few guests had left earlier, but those living close by stayed on until the end so it wasn't surprising that there wasn't much activity first thing the next morning in Cowchester Hall. In fact, when the gong sounded for breakfast, it was several minutes before anyone appeared, Michael being the last to arrive as usual! Anthony was full of chatter about the wedding and Uncle William going away on a honeymoon with Auntie Caroline.

'What time train are we catching this morning, Michael?' enquired Lord Barnes.

'It's the eleven thirty-two train, Father.'

'I must say it has been a privilege to have had William's wedding in this beautiful cathedral and to get to know a little about the area. I found it most interesting talking to some of the guests about farming in the fens. Their methods are quite different from ours, don't you think, Michael? On the train journey here, I noticed how black the soil is, and Bertram told me that when they are ploughing, they still sometimes dig up trees which are buried in the soil. Did you notice all that water on the land just before you arrived?'

'Yes, Father. Uncle Harold told us a bit about the countryside when we first got here. They grow very different crops too.'

By the time they had finished breakfast and packed their cases, it was time to say goodbye to Mrs Good and to thank Canon Fortesque for having them all to stay.

They made their way down to the station, with Anthony getting quite excited about showing his grandfather the swans on the journey back. So much so that when they boarded the train, he made a beeline for a seat by the window!

Mr Parry was at the station to collect them. Needless to say, by this time Anthony was fast asleep and Michael had to carry him off the train.

'I hope Mrs Craddock has got everything ready for us,' said Lucy.

'I'm sure she has!' replied Michael. 'She will be there to welcome us back, you'll see!'

True to form, Mrs Craddock was there waiting for them when Mr Parry arrived at the Old Gatehouse, before carrying on up to the Manor with his lordship.

'By the way, my lord, can I come to see you tomorrow morning? It concerns Mrs Druly and Matt Schulz.'

'Very well,' said Lord Barnes. 'Until tomorrow then!'

'Have you had a nice time, my lord?'

'Yes, Mrs Brookes. Though I feel quite tired after my journey.'

'Well, my lord, as far as I can see from the appointments book, there's opportunity for you to start your day a little later than usual tomorrow.'

'I might do just that, Mrs Brookes. Thank you!'

As for the happy couple, they arrived at their hotel in the highlands, tired and hungry but glad to be alone at last!

At breakfast the next morning, Mrs Craddock asked Anthony, 'Did you have a nice time at Uncle William's wedding?'

'I went on a train and saw lots of swans and I went inside the cathedral. We stayed at Uncle Harold's house. I had a bedroom all to myself, and in the night a man came and read to me.'

'That's enough, Anthony!' said Lucy.

'You must have been dreaming,' said Mrs Craddock.

'No, I wasn't!' protested Anthony.

'That's enough, Anthony. I shan't tell you again! You may get down from the table now.'

'Children dream some funny things at times, especially if they are in a strange bed,' remarked Mrs Craddock.

'Yes,' replied Lucy. 'He will keep on about it to people.'

'Well,' said Mrs Craddock, 'he will forget all about it in time, I expect! -Changing the subject, the butcher brought us a nice piece of lamb for dinner tonight, Miss Lucy.'

'Oh, that will be lovely! That's my favourite!'

'Yes, Miss Lucy, I thought you would like it. Oh -and Cook has been having trouble with the boiler again.'

'Don't worry, I will ask Michael to have a look at it to see what has to be done.'

'Thank you, Miss Lucy!'

BANG!!!

'Whatever was that, Mrs Craddock?'

'It sounds as if it came from the kitchen.'

Going to investigate, Mrs Craddock was just in time to hear Mrs Judd say, 'You naughty boy! You nearly had me down!'

'What's wrong, Mrs Judd?'

'This young scallywag kicked his football at me and it nearly had me over!'

'Anthony, come here at once! How many times must I tell you not to play football in the house?' reprimanded Lucy.

'Now you're for it my lad!' said Mrs Craddock sternly, but also trying not to laugh.

'I wish Michael had never bought him that football,' said Lucy. 'It's been a nuisance ever since he gave it to him!'

Looking out of the window, Mrs Craddock said, 'Miss Lucy, I think your father-in-law is about to call.'

'Will you show him into the drawing room, Mrs Craddock? I expect he has come to see Michael.'

'Good morning, my lord,' said Lucy.

'Good morning, Lucy. Is Michael about?'

'He's in his study, my lord.'

Hearing his grandfather's voice, Anthony came running in to see him.

'And how is my grandson this morning?' enquired Lord Barnes.

'Getting under everyone's feet!' said Lucy. 'He nearly knocked Mrs Judd down with his football this morning!'

Looking at Lucy and then Mrs Craddock, Lord Barnes said, with a smirk on his face, 'Boys like to play football!'

'I might know you would stick up for him!' laughed Lucy.

Smiling at Anthony, Lord Barnes said, 'Us men must stick together, mustn't we?'

Going into the study with Lucy to find Michael, Lord Barnes said, 'I've been thinking… Wouldn't it be nice, now we have a larger family, to invite them all to the Manor for a family get-together, say, sometime around Christmas? What do you both think about that?'

'I think it would be wonderful,' said Michael.

'So do I,' agreed Lucy.

'Perhaps you, Lucy and Caroline, would give it some thought, and when you have come up with some ideas we can meet to form a plan of action?'

'Yes, my lord, I'll have a word with Caroline as soon as she returns from her honeymoon and we'll see what we can do.'

'Now, Michael, we need to discuss the situation should Mrs Druly and Matt Schulz decide to get married. Mr Parry suggested they might live in the old gamekeeper's cottage on the far side of the wood. I know it wants a bit doing to it, but they could reside there away from the other tenants. Eventually Matt would be accepted, time is a great healer. I've been told he is a very good worker and seems to get on well with the other men on the Estate.'

'That certainly seems to be a solution,' said Michael, 'but first, we need to know for certain if the marriage will go ahead.'

'I'm still awaiting a ruling from London on that. These things take such a long time. Meanwhile, keep trying to recruit suitable workers as needed. I've also told Mr Parry to reassure those tenants whose loved ones did not return from war, that they are quite safe and will not be turned out of their homes. I hope you are in agreement?'

'I am, Father.'

Leaving the men to their discussions, Lucy returned to the drawing room where Mrs Craddock was busy tidying up.

'Have you noticed, Miss Lucy, that his lordship comes here now to see Mr Michael, rather than using the telephone?'

'Yes, I have – and I know what the reason is! By coming here, it gives his lordship a chance to see young Anthony. He idolises his grandson and would do anything for him.'

'Yes, I know, and Anthony is very fond of his grandfather. They do get on well together. Now, Miss Lucy, please excuse me, I must go and see how Mrs Judd is getting on with lunch.'

Having got things settled with Michael, Lord Barnes returned to the drawing room.

'Lucy, you will remember to speak to Caroline about the family get-together when she gets back, won't you?'

'Yes, my lord, I will. I think it would be great fun.'

'So do I,' replied his lordship.

CHAPTER 18

On returning to the Manor, Lord Barnes was met by Mrs Brookes, who informed him that she had just put the post on his desk in the study. 'Thank you, Mrs Brookes.'

Settling himself down, Lord Barnes began opening his letters. To his surprise, he found he had a letter from Professor Clifton who stated that he would like to come to see his lordship on a matter of some urgency.

'I wonder what he wants?' thought Lord Barnes.

Then the telephone rang. Picking up the receiver, he heard a voice say, 'Hello, Father, it's William! I thought I would give you a call to let you know we've arrived safely and are having a lovely time.'

'I'm so glad – it is good to hear from you!' said Lord Barnes. 'We arrived back yesterday. It was a wonderful wedding.'

'Yes, it was. I want to thank you, Father – Caroline and I are so very happy. We plan to go walking today, the scenery here is breathtaking! We'll send you a postcard later on. Must go now, goodbye, Father!'

'Goodbye, William, and thank you for calling!'

After his post-prandial nap, Lord Barnes decided to walk down to the Old Gatehouse again to tell Michael and Lucy that he had heard from William. This would also give him another chance to see his grandson.

When he arrived he was met by Mrs Craddock, who said he would find Miss Lucy and Mr Michael in the drawing room.

'I thought I would come to tell you both that I received a telephone call from William a short while ago, and he and Caroline are having a very happy time by the sounds of it. I expect I will find it strange now, not having William about the Manor, but that is something I will have to get used to! I wonder how Charles and Emily are feeling, not having Caroline at home? Now where is my grandson this afternoon?'

'Oh,' said Lucy, 'he's playing in the wash-house!'

'Well, I won't disturb him then,' said Lord Barnes. 'I must be off now as I've got Mr Parry coming to see me.'

At that, his lordship departed and almost immediately Mrs Craddock appeared, enquiring whether Miss Lucy, Mister Michael and Master Anthony would be going up to the Manor for Sunday lunch again.

'I'm not sure, Mrs Craddock. His lordship hasn't said anything yet and I didn't think to ask him when he was here. I will let you know.'

'Thank you, Miss Lucy.'

'By the way, Mrs Craddock, Anthony is still playing in the wash-house isn't he?'

'He was the last time I was that way. Would you like me to go and see?'

'Only if you have time.'

'I think Agnes is keeping an eye on him.'

'Oh, that's all right then! I don't want him getting into mischief. I'll take him out for a walk soon, that will help to make him sleep better tonight – I hope! -Oh, hello, Michael!'

'Lucy, darling, would you come into the study? I want to have a word with you.'

'I'll go and make sure young Anthony is all right, Miss Lucy.'

'Thank you, Mrs Craddock.'

Making their way into the study, Michael said, 'I have just had a telephone call from Uncle Bertram, inviting us to stay for a few days. I said I would talk it over with you and then let him know.'

'Did he say when, Michael?'

'In about three or four weeks' time. Perhaps you had better speak to him, dear?'

'All right, I will,' said Lucy.

So going over to the telephone, Lucy called Uncle Bertram, 'We would love to come and see you, Uncle, thank you for asking us. William will be back from his honeymoon in a fortnight, so we'll look forward to arranging a suitable date then.'

When the conversation was over, Lucy turned to Michael and said, 'It will be lovely to have a few days away again!'

When Lucy and Anthony had gone out for their walk to see the deer in the park, Michael spoke to his father, 'Hello, Father. Lucy has taken Anthony for a walk. They haven't been gone long and I thought I would let you know that I've been speaking to Uncle Bertram. He has invited the three of us to go and stay with him for a few days so we said we would, but not until William gets back from his honeymoon – we didn't want to leave you to manage the Estate on your own without one of us being around.'

'Thank you for your consideration and for letting me know, Michael.'

Over at Craig Lodge, Emily Fortesque remarked, 'It's so quiet without Caroline, I do miss her, Charles!'

'Yes, dear, so do I. I feel like a fish out of water now the wedding is over, Emily, if you know what I mean?'

'Well, we'll have to get used to it, she's got her own life to lead. William is a nice boy and I'm sure they will be very happy together. When all's said and done, they won't be living so very far away!'

'I'm sure we'll see them often, in any case Caroline is bound to come to see us when William is at work,' said Lord Fortesque. 'I should think Cedric will be feeling just the same as us. It's bound to feel strange even if William is working for the Estate – still, he has a grandson nearby to go and see.'

The next two weeks passed quickly and it was soon time for William and Caroline to return from their honeymoon.

Stopping the night at Craig Lodge to see Caroline's parents, they then travelled on to visit Lord Barnes the following day.

When William heard that Michael and family were going to stay at Uncle Bertram's, he asked Caroline if she minded staying with him at the Manor while his brother was away, adding that it would also give the decorators a chance to finish in their own house before they settled in. Caroline agreed, and Lord Barnes was delighted to know that he would be having company during this time.

On hearing this, Lucy was keen to exchange news with Caroline and to talk over Lord Barnes' idea of a family get-together, so wasted no time in arranging to meet on the day that William and Caroline were to arrive.

The ladies spent considerable time together – firstly talking about the wedding and the honeymoon, before moving on to discuss what form the family gathering would take. Caroline agreed to check everyone's availability and to organise invitations. Hopefully they could settle on a date which would be acceptable for everyone and there might also be an idea of numbers by the time Michael and Lucy returned from Uncle Bertram's.

Lord Barnes was delighted to hear their ideas and gave his consent for them to put plans into operation straightaway.

Lucy said to Caroline, 'Well, that seems to be everything – we will be leaving after breakfast tomorrow morning for Uncle Bertram's.'

'Will you give him my love? He has always been so kind to me and such good fun to be with. I know you will enjoy your time there!'

'I'm looking forward to going, Caroline. Mrs Craddock and I haven't started to pack yet, but I won't take much in the way of clothes.'

'Don't forget to take your wellington boots though, you will need them!' laughed Caroline.

That evening, Michael and Lucy were busy checking their cases to make sure everything had been packed. As usual, Anthony was asking all sorts of questions about where they were going to stay and who they were going to meet, until Michael said to Anthony, 'I expect Uncle Bertram will want you to ride on the bull!'

There was silence.

Then Lucy said, 'Don't tease him, Michael! We will have enough to do without being up half the night trying to get him to sleep!'

CHAPTER 19

The following day, Michael, Lucy and Anthony boarded the train to Wentley village station, not far from Uncle Bertram's house. They were met by Arnold Fortesque, who welcomed them and drove them to the farmhouse.

Aunt Annie was waiting to greet them and said, 'I'm so pleased you could come. Bertram will be home soon – he's looking forward to seeing you again, as indeed are we all. Come on in and I will show you to your room and then I'll put the kettle on!'

Looking down at Anthony, Aunt Annie said, 'Mary

has gone to get some ice-cream for tea. I know little boys like ice-cream.'

A broad grin appeared on Anthony's face, and letting go of his mother's hand he said, 'I like ice-cream!'

'I thought you would !' replied Aunt Annie.

Turning to Michael, Arnold asked, 'Michael, do you shoot?'

'Whenever I get the chance.'

'Well, we must try to get some in while you are here.'

'That will be splendid!' responded Michael, enthusiastically.

'Ah! That sounds like Mary back,' said Aunt Annie. 'I'll let her look after you while I put the kettle on.'

Walking into the room, Mary said to Anthony, 'I've been to get you something nice for your tea!'

'I like ice-cream!' replied Anthony.

'Oh, you know where I've been then!' chuckled Mary. 'Well, did my mother also tell you that we are going to have strawberries for tea as well?'

'Oooh!' said Michael, 'I'm going to like being here!'

'Anyone would think you'd never had strawberries before, dear!'

'I can always eat strawberries – I do like them!'

'Yes,' said Lucy, 'I know you do!'

Just then, Aunt Annie came in with the tea-tray, and putting it down on the table said, 'I expect Bert won't be long. He's looking forward to having a chat with Michael about the farm on his father's estate.'

'I think I can hear Peter, so Father won't be far behind,' said Mary. 'They usually arrive home about the same time.'

It was Peter who came into the room first, 'Hello everyone, did you have a good journey?'

'Yes, thank you,' replied Lucy, 'and aren't we fortunate with the weather?'

'Hello!' said Uncle Bertram, 'It's nice to see you all again!'

Looking at Anthony, Peter said, 'We've got a nanny goat for you to ride on!'

Anthony said, 'Daddy told me I was going to ride on the bull!'

Everyone started to laugh, but it was Uncle Bertram who came to the rescue by saying, 'Your Daddy can ride on the bull because he's got longer legs, but I've got a nice little pony, just waiting for someone like you to ride on it – and as for Peter here, I will put him on the largest old horse I can find, for teasing you! Goats are funny animals, you had best keep away from them, they will eat anything they get near.'

Anthony was by now looking very perplexed and went to hide behind his mother, but Uncle Bertram soon reassured him that everything would be all right!

Then the conversation amongst the men turned to farming, so Mary said to Lucy, 'It was lovely everyone meeting up at the wedding. I understand you and Caroline are arranging a family get-together before Christmas?'

'Yes, Mary, we are. Lord Barnes thought it would be a wonderful opportunity for all the family to get better acquainted and we do hope you will all be able to come.'

'Well, if you would like another pair of hands to help with preparations, just let me know.'

'That's very good of you, Mary,' said Lucy, 'I'll certainly do so.'

After supper, Uncle Bertram said, 'How about a singsong, Mother?'

Anthony found this very amusing since Uncle Bertram kept singing the wrong words and pulling funny faces at him. By the time it was nine o'clock, Lucy said , 'I think it's time you were in bed, young man.'

Anthony did not object as he usually did because he had been told he was sleeping in a bed in the attic, which was reserved for special people. This made him feel very important, and when he was told Uncle William had slept in that very bed, he could not get there fast enough!

When Lucy returned downstairs, Arnold asked, 'How did you get on staying at Uncle Harold's?'

'Very well, thank you, but I found the house had a strange feeling about it. Uncle Harold made us very welcome though.'

'Yes, he is a kind man. Did he show you around the cathedral, Lucy?'

'Yes, Arnold, we had a good look round. It's amazing to think they could build something like that all those years ago.'

'I could tell you a story about Uncle Harold's house because I have worked there!'

'Oh,' said Michael, suddenly latching on to the conversation, 'What?'

'Well…' said Arnold.

At this point, Uncle Bertram stood up and asked, 'Who would like a glass of wine – or would you rather have a glass of beer, Michael?'

'Sit down, dear,' said his wife, 'you have been at work all day. I will see to the drinks.'

Lucy said, 'Michael, will you go and say goodnight to Anthony? He's very tired tonight, it's a bit later than his normal bedtime.'

Michael made his way to the attic, only to find his son fast asleep. Bending over, he gave him a goodnight kiss and quietly left the room.

CHAPTER 20

As they were making their way down to breakfast, Michael said to Lucy, 'I feel quite hungry – it must be this fenland air!'

'Yes,' said Lucy, 'I feel hungry myself.'

'I'm hungry too!' piped up a little voice.

'You're always hungry!' teased Michael.

'I'm glad to hear that!' said Aunt Annie, coming into the dining room with a plate of bacon, fried eggs, mushrooms and tomatoes, and setting it down in front of Lucy.

'My word, that smells good!' gasped Lucy.

Michael quipped, 'You'll do well, dear, if you eat all that!'

Not wishing to disappoint Aunt Annie, she said, 'I'll do my best!'

Aunt Annie then returned with an even larger plate and said, 'Try this, Michael!' putting it down in front of him.

'My goodness, I shall be here until lunchtime with all this!'

'But Uncle Bertram said I could go riding this morning,' said a little voice.

'Don't worry, Anthony, you'll be able to go after you have had your breakfast!'

'-And here it is!' smiled Aunt Annie.

'Is it far to walk to the farmyard?' enquired Lucy.

'No, about ten minutes away.'

'I'll come with you too,' said Mary.

'Uncle Bertram said I must keep away from the nanny goat because they do funny things to you,' said Anthony.

Michael laughed, 'Funny things, eh? I once got butted by a goat and I've never forgotten it!'

Lucy laughed, 'Were you able to sit down afterwards?'

'Not for a while!' chortled Michael.

Breakfast over, Michael and Lucy, together with Mary and Anthony, made their way down to the farm to find Uncle Bertram. He was working with Peter in the barn. Peter said, 'Would you like to have a ride on the goat, Anthony?'

'I'll put you on the goat, Peter, if you don't stop teasing him. Go and get Biscuit out of the stable for Anthony to ride.'

Anthony said, 'Can I go too?' and before Lucy could stop him, Anthony ran over to Peter, taking hold of his hand as they walked off to find Biscuit.

'He's happy now!' said Michael.

'I hope Peter holds on to him,' said Lucy.

'He'll be all right! Peter may be a bit of a tease, but he'll take great care to see Anthony is safe,' replied Uncle Bertram, reassuringly.

Five minutes later, Biscuit appeared, being led by George Halfsharp, with Anthony proudly sitting on the pony's back, and Peter holding on to him in case he should fall.

'Look, Mummy! Peter said whenever I come here, I will be able to ride on this pony. Can I have a pony of my own, Daddy please?'

'Well, we'll have to see what we can do, Anthony.'

Mary said, 'When you're old enough to ride by yourself, you can come riding with Auntie Caroline and me if you like!'

'Lucy, do you ride?' asked Uncle Bertram.

'Sometimes, Uncle, when I can. It's a little difficult – the horses are stabled a good half an hour away from our house and by the time I've got there and back, it doesn't seem worth the trouble.'

When it was time for lunch, Lucy went to find Anthony who was still riding around with Peter holding on to him.

'We must go now, dear, Auntie is expecting us for lunch.'

'Just a little longer!' pleaded Anthony.

'Peter has got his work to do! He can't keep holding on to you all day while you are sitting there enjoying yourself!'

Reluctantly, he let Peter lift him down, and holding his mother's hand, the pair of them went to find Michael.

Lucy said to Anthony, 'Did you say 'thank you' to Peter for holding you on the pony?...... I thought not!'

Just then, Peter appeared, 'Thank you, Uncle Peter, for the ride. Can I come again, please?'

'Yes, of course you can,' replied Peter, 'whenever your mummy and daddy can bring you.'

Feeling pleased with himself, Anthony joined his mother and father in thanking Uncle Bertram for showing them round.

After lunch, Anthony said, 'Can we go back to the farm this afternoon, Mummy?'

'I don't know,' said his mother, 'we'll have to see!'

Mary, seeing Lucy's face, said, 'Anthony, I want to ask your mother to help me with something this afternoon. Couldn't you play with your toys?'

'I'll take him,' said Michael, 'when I've had a bit of a nap!'

It wasn't long before Anthony got his way, and together father and son set off once more for the farm. As they passed the barn, they saw George Halfsharp working on a chaff cutter.

'Is Peter here, George?'

'No, Mr Michael. He's helping the master in the little fields this afternoon.'

'Oh, that's a pity,' said Michael, looking at his son, 'but there'll be another day when you can go riding, Anthony. It looks like you've got yourself a job there, George!'

'Yes, I can't make out what is wrong with it!'

Going over to see what George was doing, Michael said, 'Shall I have a look at it?'

While Michael and George were busy trying to find the trouble, Anthony, tired of waiting around, wandered off further into the farmyard. Walking past the straw stack, he saw the ducks swimming on the pond. Being attracted to water, as most boys are, he went over to have a closer look. Then catching sight of the geese having their afternoon nap, he took a step towards them. Immediately the gander got up and with wings flapping, neck outstretched and hissing loudly, it ran towards Anthony who took fright. Turning quickly to run away, he slipped on some mud and fell into the water with a splash, which sent the ducks scurrying off the pond, quacking loudly!

Michael, hearing cries of 'Help!' hurried to find his son, who by then was emerging from the pond, covered in duckweed!

'Oh, Anthony, are you all right?'

'That g-g-goose came after me!' wailed Anthony.

Seeing his son was none the worse for wear and taking hold of a wet little hand, Michael said, 'You do look a sight – whatever your mother will say, I don't know! The main thing is you're not hurt, but we must get you out of those soggy, wet clothes as soon as possible!'

As father and son hurried past the barn, George, seeing the boy in distress, called out, 'Is the lad all right, Mister Michael?'

'Yes, I think so, George – the gander went for him!'

'Oh,' said George, trying not to laugh, 'he goes for most folk if they go near the geese!'

When Michael and Anthony arrived back, Mary saw them first.

'Whatever has happened to Anthony?'

Michael said, 'He was chased by the gander and fell in the pond!'

'Oh,' said Mary, trying not to laugh.

Then Aunt Annie came into the kitchen. 'Sakes alive! What's happened to you, my boy?'

Hearing all the commotion, Lucy came into the room, 'Anthony, whatever have you been up to? Oh, Michael, fancy letting him get in that state. You should have taken more care of him!'

'Yes, I'm afraid it was my fault,' said Michael. 'I was having a look at the chaff cutter with George Halfsharp, and Anthony wandered off. Seeing the ducks on the pond, he went over to look. It was then that the gander went for him, and in his haste to get away, Anthony slipped and fell into the water!'

By now, all three women were having a job not to laugh – even Lucy, who at first was cross with Michael – could now see the funny side of it. Turning away to regain her composure, she said, 'I had better get him in a bath!'

Then, putting her arm around him, she took her bedraggled son to get him cleaned up.

When they had gone, Mary said to Michael, 'I was chased by that gander once and ever since then I've kept away from the geese!' Still chuckling to herself she added, 'Never mind, Michael, I think Lucy will forgive you! After the initial shock, even she could see the funny side of it!'

When Uncle Bertram and Peter came in for supper, they were concerned for Anthony, as George Halfsharp was only able to tell them that Anthony had fallen into the pond. But when they saw him playing happily with his toys, none the worse for his exploits at the farm, they were very relieved and asked exactly what had happened.

Then they were told the full story, and throughout the course of the evening, one after another could be heard chuckling at the thought of Anthony falling into the pond!

CHAPTER 21

As Michael and Lucy made their way upstairs, Lucy asked, 'By the way, Michael, was it this week that Mrs Warboys was visiting your father?'

'Yes, it was,' he replied. 'He seemed to have taken a fancy to her at William's wedding, but I don't think there's anything in it!'

'You never can tell, still waters run deep! I once thought Mrs Brookes had her eye on your father,' said Lucy.

'Oh, no! He would not encourage anything with her. He only sees her as a good and loyal housekeeper.'

'Well,' said Lucy, 'with William married, your father will be alone in the Manor now. He might be thinking it would be nice to have someone living there with him.'

'I must say, Mrs Warboys is quite an attractive woman!' said Michael.

'You've got a wife!' teased Lucy. 'Come on, it's time for bed!'

The next morning, Anthony was keen to get down to breakfast.

'And how are you this morning, young man, after your visit to the farm yesterday?' asked Aunt Annie, who was busy setting the table.

'I'm very well, thank you, Auntie.'

'And what are you going to do today then?'

'I don't know,' replied Anthony. His face suddenly lit up, 'Can I go riding again today, Daddy, please?'

'We'll have to see,' said Michael.

'I'm glad he's none the worse for wear after yesterday's exploits,' said Aunt Annie, with a smile.

'No,' said Michael, 'but I think he will keep well away from the geese in future!'

The next few days were uneventful. Anthony managed to get another ride on Biscuit, and a congenial time was had by everyone.

All too soon it was time for Michael and family to leave.

'Don't forget, if you need any help with the get-together, just let me know and I will come,' Mary offered.

After saying goodbye, Arnold took Michael, Lucy and Anthony to the station, to embark upon their homeward journey across the fens.

'It's good to have you back!' said Mrs Craddock. 'It seemed strangely quiet not having young Anthony about the place. I hope you all had a nice time.'

'Yes, we did, thank you, Mrs Craddock. Has everything been all right here?'

'Yes, Miss Lucy. Lord Barnes was anxious to know when you were coming back, so I expect you will be getting a visit from him today!'

Sure enough, it wasn't long before Lord Barnes arrived, and when he heard that Anthony had been on a pony, it gave him an idea – although he didn't say anything at the time. Turning to Michael, he asked, 'Could I have a word with you in your study?'

'Yes, Father, follow me!'

Closing the door behind them, Lord Barnes said, 'I've received a letter concerning Matt Schulz, stating that there was some confusion over whether he was free to marry Mrs Druly, so I have asked her to make an appointment to see me at her earliest convenience. I thought you ought to know immediately how things stood, Michael.'

'Thank you, Father.'

Two weeks went by, and one morning, Lord Barnes telephoned Michael and Lucy to say he had something at the

Manor for Anthony. When they went up to see what it was, they were surprised to see a pony standing outside with Tim, one of the farmworkers. As they stood admiring it, Lord Barnes appeared and as soon as Anthony saw his grandfather, he ran over to him and was scooped up and whirled around before being asked, 'Would you like to have a ride on this pony?'

'Ooh, yes please, Grandfather.'

Anthony couldn't get on quickly enough. Lifting him on to the pony's back, Lord Barnes said to Tim, 'Just walk him around to see how he likes it!'

After five minutes or so, Lord Barnes said, 'Anthony, this is your pony, and whenever your Mummy or Daddy can spare the time to bring you here to ride him, they just have to let me know and I will see he is ready!'

Anthony was beside himself!

'We can't thank you enough, Father,' said Michael.

'That is so kind of you,' said Lucy. 'As you know, Anthony has been on a pony at Uncle Bertram's, in fact he had three rides on it! This is a lovely pony – you've made him a very happy boy,' said Lucy.

'Good, I hope he will get a lot of pleasure riding it,' said Lord Barnes.

For the rest of the day, Anthony could talk of nothing but the pony which his kind grandfather had bought him!

After several journeys back and forth to the Manor – which kept Tim busy all afternoon – Anthony asked,

'Daddy, why can't I have my pony here at home? Then I could ride him every day.'

'Well, Anthony, we haven't got a place to keep a pony, besides, who would feed it and keep his stable clean? Ponies have to be looked after very carefully, and on the farm, Tim can see that your pony is fed and cared for properly, ready for you whenever you want to ride it. You are a very lucky boy, Anthony, to have a pony all for yourself! I didn't have one until I was grown up!'

Anthony didn't give Michael or Lucy – or Tim – much rest during the coming weeks. All he could talk about was his pony, and when could he go up to his grandfather's to ride it? After several days of this, they managed to get Anthony into a routine, going three times a week. Even then, his conversation was almost entirely centred on his pony, which he called Rufus.

One morning, Lucy telephoned Caroline to say she thought they ought to start making arrangements for the December weekend. Lord Barnes had offered the use of a room at the Manor where they could work, and Caroline had been told that she was welcome to stay there while all this was going on. With Lucy about to spend more time up at the Manor, Michael had the job of looking after Anthony once he had finished lessons, which meant that the staff were in for a lively time – trying to do their work while a six year old was making hay, kicking a football around and getting into all sorts of mischief!

It came to a climax one day, when Mrs Judd bent down to pick up the laundry basket in the wash-house. Anthony kicked his football straight at her and hit her on her back-side, nearly knocking her off-balance.

'You naughty boy!' she cried. 'I will tell your mother about you and she will stop you from going riding!'

Anthony was a bit taken aback on hearing this. He looked forward to his rides. Then, when he had had a few moments to think about it, he said he was sorry to Mrs Judd – though secretly he was very proud of hitting his target!

When Michael arrived home after seeing Nigel at the farm, he heard all about Mrs Judd's brush with his son. Telling Anthony it was dangerous and unkind to kick a football at people, he added, 'You will only go riding twice next week instead of three times.'

Later on that afternoon, when Lucy arrived back from the Manor, she heard all about Anthony's encounter with Mrs Judd and made him go and apologise one more time.

CHAPTER 22

After supper, when they were on their own, Lucy said to Michael, 'We really must do something to stop our son playing football in the house. Can't a fence be put round the outside of the washhouse so he can kick the ball against the wall or something?'

'I'll have a word with Mr Parry,' said Michael.

Lucy yawned, 'Oh, I really am tired, it won't be long before I'm off to bed!'

'You shouldn't be working so hard up at the Manor with Caroline, you should be looking after yourself.'

'That's all right, dear, we've nearly finished getting it all arranged, and then I will be able to take things a little easier. We will be sending the invitations out very soon. Your father has asked us to invite Mrs Warboys -and she'll be staying for the weekend! I told you I thought something was going on there with that woman!'

'Well, Father hasn't said anything to me about it,' replied Michael. 'He's a bit of a dark horse, my father!'

'Well, time will tell,' said Lucy. 'There could be as many as fifteen of us in all that weekend, so we should have a jolly time. I hope Uncle Harold will be able to stay until the Sunday and isn't needed in the cathedral.'

Next morning, Lucy reminded Michael that she had a meeting at the Manor at ten o'clock with his father and Caroline, and that she hoped he would be able to keep an eye on Anthony while she was there. About the time this conversation was taking place at the Old Gatehouse, there was an unexpected visitor at Caiston Manor, which prompted Mrs Brookes to tap on the study door announcing, 'Mrs Druly is here to see you, my lord.'

'Show her in, Mrs Brookes.'

'Come in, Mrs Druly, and take a seat.'

'Thank you, my lord. I thought I had better come to see you to explain what has happened since I had the official report that my Joe had been killed in the war.

I was putting the washing out one morning when the clothes line broke. It so happened that the German workers were busy in the field at the bottom of my garden, and one of them came over to the fence to ask if he could be of any help, and so I said that my line had broken and he, being a handy sort of person, repaired it for me. From that day on, we became friends.

My youngest girl has taken to him as though he was her father but my other daughter, being older and still remembering Joe before he went away, is rather suspicious of him. Anyway, he seems a nice man and speaks English well in spite of him being a German. He has told me he is not married and likes working here on the Estate.'

'Yes,' said Lord Barnes, 'Mr Parry has spoken well of him. He is a good workman.'

'Well, my lord, we have become close friends and I wondered – if we were to marry – would we be able to remain in my cottage?'

'Has he asked you, Mrs Druly?'

'Not in so many words, my lord.'

'Well,' said Lord Barnes, 'I can't see why not, providing the authorities are happy – he being a German, but how would your neighbours feel, living next door to you? Would you lose your friends if you did marry him? I don't want the other tenants upset. Having said that, I have a suggestion to make, Mrs Druly: the gamekeeper's old cottage, on the far side of the Estate, is empty at the moment. It wants a bit of fixing up, but you would be quite all right there. What do you think?'

'Thank you, my lord, that sounds perfect. Please don't think I have forgotten about my husband. He was a good-living man and I shall always love him, but thinking about my two children, they really could do with a man about the house to help me care for them.'

'Well, Mrs Druly, I must leave you to decide what's best. I know you can't do much until the powers-that-be approve any request to marry, but as far as I am concerned – whatever the outcome – I will not stand in your way, and will help you to get settled.'

'Thank you so much, my lord, for being so helpful and for sparing the time to see me.'

'Well,' said Lord Barnes, 'I have another appointment in five minutes, so I must bid you good day, Mrs Druly.'

'Good day, my lord.'

'Mrs Brookes will see you out.'

Just as Mrs Druly was leaving, Lucy arrived, and joining Caroline, they both went into the study to see Lord Barnes.

About an hour and a half later, Lucy said, 'To sum up then, we will send out the invitations tomorrow, and as your lordship has agreed, we think it's a good idea to involve Mrs Brookes and Mrs Craddock to order the extra food required. As soon as we get the replies back, we will give Mrs Brookes the list of those who will be staying at the Manor so she knows how many rooms to prepare.'

'Excellent!' said Lord Barnes. 'You have both done well. By the way, your idea of asking each person to think of a story they could tell during the weekend, whether true or fictitious, would cause a certain amount of amusement, and then we could vote on who has told the best story. It could be a lot of fun!'

'Thank you, my lord, that's just what we thought!'

'Yes, it sounds most entertaining!'

Looking at her watch, Lucy said, 'Well, I think I should get back now and see what mischief your grandson has been up to, so I'll say goodbye to you both!'

As she was leaving the Manor, she saw William.

'Hello, Lucy! Is Caroline there?'

'Yes, William. I have just left her with his lordship. You'll find her inside.'

Making his way through the hall, he saw Caroline coming away from the study.

'Hello, my darling! I thought I would come to see how you were getting on.'

'We've only just finished,' said Caroline, 'we will be sending the invitations out tomorrow.'

'Does this mean after tomorrow we will be able to return home?'

'I hope so,' said Caroline.

Just then, Mrs Brookes came into the hall and seeing Caroline she said, 'As soon as you've heard who's coming, will you please let me know? I have a certain amount of juggling to do to get everyone in!'

Assuring Mrs Brookes that this would be the case, and then bidding her good day, William and Caroline set off for the Old Gatehouse where William wanted to have a word with his brother.

'I wonder how my nephew is this morning?' smiled William.

'Lucy told me he'd been a naughty boy!'

'Oh,' said William, 'what's he been doing now?'

'He kicked his football at Mrs Judd and it hit her on the you-know-what, nearly knocking her over!' giggled Caroline.

'Poor Anthony!' laughed William, 'I bet he got a good telling off for that!'

'Poor Anthony! – You mean poor Mrs Judd!' replied Caroline. 'If she had fallen down at her age, she could have seriously hurt herself. As it was, no harm was done! He seems to be having quite a time of it at the moment. Lucy was telling me that when they were away at Uncle Bertram's, Anthony was chased by the gander and fell into the pond. Lucy said she had to put him in the bath to get him clean – he was very smelly and covered in duckweed!'

By this time, William was beside himself laughing, 'This gets better all the time!' he said. 'When we have children, I suppose we must be prepared for this sort of thing, although if they do fall into the duck pond, does it really matter so long as they're not hurt?'

'No,' said Caroline, laughing, 'providing you do all the clearing up afterwards!'

CHAPTER 23

'Is Michael about?' William enquired when he and Caroline arrived at the Old Gatehouse.

'He's in his study,' called a voice.

'Oh, thank you, Mrs Craddock! Has he got anyone with him?'

'Only Miss Lucy. Would you like me to tell him you want to see him?'

'Yes, please, Mrs Craddock.'

'Hello, William! I thought I heard your voice,' said Michael, coming into the hall. 'Did you want to see me?'

'Yes, Michael.'

Lucy appeared and said, '-And while you two are talking, Caroline and I have something to discuss. Let's go into the drawing room, Caroline – I've something to ask you!'

Once they were both settled, Lucy said, 'Michael and I are thinking of having a holiday in the Spring, and from what you have told us, we rather like the sound of Scotland. What was it like where you were staying?'

'I can show you some of the postcards we brought back, if you like? I have them in an album at home.'

'Thank you, that would be lovely. I had hoped to have some good news to tell you today, but it was a false alarm! We would dearly love to have a brother or sister for Anthony to play with but...' Lucy yawned, 'Oh, dear, I'm sorry, I do get so tired! There's always so much to do!'

'It's a good thing we have Mary's help with the get-together then, you mustn't overdo it!' said Caroline.

'You sound just like Michael!' said Lucy, pulling a face.

'I wonder if Anthony will think he's going on a honeymoon when he knows he may be going up to Scotland for a holiday?' giggled Caroline.

'Oh, we won't be telling him anything yet!'

'-By the way, where is Anthony?'

'I sent him off to play with his toys in his room where I hope he can come to no harm!'

Just then, Mrs Craddock put her head round the door and asked how many there would be for lunch.

'Will you both stay, Caroline?' asked Lucy.

'That's kind, yes, please!'

'In that case, Mrs Craddock, there will be five.'

Four weeks had passed, and Lucy and Caroline had received all the replies to the family weekend invitations, so Lucy had been able to give Mrs Brookes a list of all those staying. It was going to be a full house, and as the weekend drew near, the Great Hall was decorated with festive garlands and a very large Christmas tree, under which there were presents for everyone.

A week before the party weekend, Lucy decided to take Anthony with her after breakfast when she went up to the Manor, but she soon found it was a mistake as he got into all sorts of mischief, so she had to take him home again – much to the disappointment of his grandfather!

In the afternoon, Mary arrived to help, and during the evening, when they were all relaxing after dinner, Mary was telling Lucy about a recent visit from the vicar.

'Last week, the vicar called. He was collecting for the church roof fund. Dad has always helped the church if he could, and since this was rather an urgent case – with the roof letting in water, he said he would see what he could do. The vicar then went on to say, 'You've been to a wedding in Beeley recently, haven't you?' I replied that we all went and that it had been my cousin's wedding. I mentioned that some of the family had stayed with Uncle Harold at his home. 'Oh!' said the vicar. 'Once I stayed with your Uncle Harold – when all the clergy attended a confirmation service – but I wouldn't stay there again. It's a strange house and has an unsettling atmosphere. I was glad when I could leave, although your Uncle made me very welcome.'

I thought after the vicar had gone, you and Michael stayed there didn't you? Did you find anything untoward?'

'No,' said Lucy. 'We all slept well. Anthony kept telling us funny stories but he must have dreamt those up! You know how young children imagine things. I must say, your Uncle gave up a lot of his time to ensure we enjoyed our visit, especially taking us round the cathedral. He will be staying here this weekend, so I will make sure he is well looked after.'

At last it was Friday – the day everyone had been looking forward to, and throughout the morning the guests arrived at the Manor. Lord Barnes, Michael and William were there to welcome them and Mrs Brookes was kept busy showing everyone to their rooms. She said, 'I have lost count of the number of times I have been up and down those stairs, Florence! It looks as if we're in for quite a time of it!'

Just before lunch, Lucy and Anthony arrived. As soon as Anthony saw his grandfather, he ran over to him and gave him a hug.

'And how is my grandson, this fine morning?'

'Very well, thank you, Grandfather.'

'I hear you have been giving Mrs Judd a hard time again! You must try to be kind to her Anthony, for when all's said and done, it's Mrs Judd who cooks your lovely food for you! Anyway, run along and enjoy yourself!'

Turning to Lucy, Lord Barnes said, 'I think everyone has arrived and most are downstairs, ready for lunch!'

'All except Uncle Bertram and family,' said Lucy, looking at the list. 'They've not come down yet.'

'Ah! Who's that now?' said Lord Barnes.

'That's them,' said Lucy. 'Now we can begin!'

Lord Barnes ushered Uncle Bertram and his family into the Great Hall. As soon as Uncle Bertram caught sight of Anthony, he went over and asked him if he'd been falling into any more ponds!

'No, Uncle Bertram, I haven't! It was very smelly and I didn't like it one bit!' squealed Anthony, stamping his foot. Everything fell quiet at this outburst, so Lord Barnes quickly stepped in, taking the opportunity to say how pleased he was to see everyone and to announce that lunch was ready.

Soon there were fifteen people seated around the table in the Great Hall, with Lord Barnes at one end and Lord Fortesque at the other. Seated next to Lord Barnes on one side was Hilda Warboys, who looked quite at home next to his lordship. On the other side was Lady Fortesque, who throughout the meal was finding it difficult to get Lord Barnes' attention!

Once lunch was over, they all moved into the drawing room while the table in the Great Hall was being cleared and moved to make way for games and dancing later in the day.

Lucy was engaged in conversation with Aunt Annie, when Peter came over to say that he had just seen Anthony having fun in the hall.

'What kind of fun?' asked Lucy.

'Well, I don't want to get him into trouble, but he was having a fine old time sliding down the bannister!'

'What?' said Lucy.

'Shall I go and get him for you?'

'Yes, please,' said Lucy.

Going into the hall, Peter said, 'Anthony, your mother is looking for you, come with me and I will take you to her. We're going to have some fun playing games soon and you wouldn't want to miss that, would you?'

CHAPTER 24

The rest of the day until dinner, was spent talking and playing games, which Anthony thoroughly enjoyed, but although a big fuss was made of him, he tried to escape whenever he could to have another go at sliding down the bannisters.

Later, when the music started for dancing, Anthony liked to sit and watch his mother and father twirl round and round the dance floor, and the antics of Peter and Uncle Bertram made him laugh!

This went on until it was well past Anthony's bedtime, when Mrs Craddock – who had been helping Mrs Brookes behind the scenes – asked Lucy if it was time for her to take Anthony back to the Old Gatehouse and put him to bed.

'Thank you, Mrs Craddock,' said Lucy, gratefully, 'but you had better take him to say goodnight to his grandfather before you leave!'

Dancing continued for some time afterwards, but by midnight, everyone was glad to make their way upstairs with the exception of Michael and Lucy, who made their way back to the Old Gatehouse.

Saturday morning breakfast lasted longer than usual and the guests were only just finishing by the time Lucy, Michael and Anthony arrived at the Manor, followed shortly afterwards by Mr and Mrs Fanshaw, who were also joining in the day's festivities.

Caroline had been talking to Peter and Arnold about the places she and William had visited on their honeymoon, but on seeing Lucy, Caroline beckoned her over to ask, 'Shall we remind everyone now that they should be ready to tell their story this evening?'

'Yes,' said Lucy, who then proceeded to do just that, ending, '…and the person who tells the best story will receive a prize.'

Lord Barnes, who had been chatting to Mrs Warboys, turned to Michael and said quietly, 'Shall we leave our discovery of the tunnel out of this game?'

'Yes, Father, I've already thought of something else!'

During the afternoon, Lucy said, 'Now, will you all gather round the Christmas tree, please? – There is a present for everyone.'

One by one the parcels were handed out. Anthony couldn't undo his present fast enough, and when he had torn off all the paper he found a toy motor car and immediately sat down on the floor to play with it.

When Lucy handed Peter his present, she looked across to Caroline with a broad grin on her face. Everyone looked on as Peter started to unwrap his rather large parcel. Layer after layer of wrapping paper was removed and Peter became more and more impatient until finally, standing in a mound of paper, he held up a bright red handkerchief. Looking at Lucy, he said, 'Someone has been playing a joke on me!' This made everyone laugh!

All too soon it was teatime and Uncle Harold said to Lord Barnes, 'Thank you so much for arranging this family get-together. I've thoroughly enjoyed myself, but I must take my leave of you all now as I am needed for the early service tomorrow morning in the cathedral.'

After saying his farewells, he departed to catch the train home.

Dinner over, the guests left the dining room and entered the Great Hall, now in semi-darkness. As instructed by Lucy, each one took a piece of paper with a number on it from a bowl – this would determine the order in which each guest would be asked to tell his or her story. The chairs had been arranged in a circle.

When everyone was seated, Lucy asked, 'Who's got number one?'

'I have!' said Lord Barnes. 'My story is about my visit to Egypt. One day, when we were digging down in the sand, trying to find the entrance to a tomb, we dug up a cross. It was about four inches long and made of gold. One of the men doing the digging bent down to pick it up and as soon as he did so, he dropped it again, falling over on to the sand, a dead man.' Everyone gasped. 'The hand he used had withered away. -Well,' said Lord Barnes, 'that's my story,' he paused for dramatic effect, '- but it's not true!'

There was a sigh of relief and everyone clapped.

Lucy said, 'Now, who has got number two?'

'I have!' said Peter. 'My story is about school holidays. One day, three of us boys went camping in one of Father's fields. My mother packed me up half a loaf of bread which had the middle cut out, and a lump of butter and some cheese put in its place. I also had a bottle of lemonade and some biscuits. Then I was ready to go. The other boys had similar packings-up. After we had secured our tent, we went birdsnesting and made bows and arrows. In the evening, when it started to get dark, the field took on a very different look, and as the mist came rolling across the ground, the night time creatures appeared. Then we became aware of all the sounds – the hoot of an owl or the screech of a fox, to say nothing of occasional sneezes from the horses in the next field. All this didn't help when you were trying to get off to sleep! But when we woke up the next morning, we found the tent under which we had been sleeping had gone! My brother and his friends had had fun by carefully removing the tent without waking us! It was a good thing it was a warm night. Well, that's my story,' said Peter, 'and it's true!'

Everyone clapped and looked at Arnold, who laughed!

'Who has number three?' Lucy asked.

'I have,' replied Uncle Bertram, standing up. 'Now, let's see…. One day, just before I left school, I went on a paperchase in the fens. I and another boy were the hares and the rest of the school, after a short delay, had to chase after us to try to catch us before we could get back to where we started. It was great fun, I can tell you! Well,' said Uncle Bertram, 'Charlie – that's the other boy – and I, were running across a field, scattering paper as we went, when suddenly we came across a herd of cows with a bull, and seeing us running, the bull wanted nothing better than to run after us. Charlie ran one way, I ran another, straight for the hedge, hoping to find a gap to get over. As the bull had to choose which of us to go for, he unfor-tunately picked me. Seeing a place in the hedge which had been repaired before, I made for that, and only just in time to avoid being tossed over it by Mr Bull! In my eagerness to escape from my pursuer, I tore the seat of my trousers on some barbed wire which had obviously been used to mend the hedge earlier. Looking up, I realised I was sitting in a flowerbed in someone's garden and as I started to walk up the path, a lady came out of the house and asked me what I was doing there. Feeling a bit embarrassed, and trying to cover a large expanse of flesh with my hand, I told her what had happened! Then she said, with an amused look on her face, 'You had better come into the house and I will find you a safety pin for your trousers.' Thanking the lady for helping me, I went on to find Charlie, who had managed to leave the field – by the gate!'

After the applause had died down, Uncle Bertram said, 'And that really did happen!'

Then Lucy said, 'Who's got number four?'

'I have!' said a little voice. It was Anthony!

Lucy stood up and said, 'In view of what happened on Uncle Bertram's farm a little while ago, we all know about you falling in the pond, so I think we can say that was a true story! Is there anything else you would like to say, Anthony?'

'Yes, I would! I didn't like being chased by the gander, but I did like having a ride on Biscuit. Please can I go again?' With that, he sat down, feeling very proud of himself! There were smiles all round!

'Now, number five?'

'That's me!' said Hilda Warboys. 'My story is a strange one but I will tell it all the same. When my late husband and I were in Egypt, we were invited by some friends of ours to see inside one of the tombs. They had been excavating there for some time and had finally reached the burial chamber. Full of excitement, my husband and I joined our friends at the site and one by one we followed the guide down into the tomb. I was more interested in the hieroglyphics on the walls of the tomb, but my husband wanted to see inside the burial chamber. Suddenly, before my husband could take his turn, a man behind us pushed in front and on looking inside, gasped, clutching his throat. He reeled round to us with a terrified look on his face and collapsed in a heap on the floor, never to speak again. The sight of that face has haunted me ever since!'

Taking a deep breath she said, 'That's my story – and it's true.'

Nobody clapped and nobody spoke. An uneasy silence prevailed until Lucy asked briskly, 'Now, who's got number six?'

Mary stood up. 'Two years ago, I went ice-skating on the Washes with some friends. It was a cold and crisp sunny morning and somehow I managed to skate away from the others and found myself quite alone. Suddenly the ice broke around me and I fell through. Following some way behind me was my very own Prince Charming, who came to my rescue, lifting me out of the water and carrying me on to dry land – and he is taking me to the pictures next Saturday!'

There was a lot of laughter following Mary's story. Then Uncle Bertram said, 'Two winters ago it was very

143

mild and we didn't have any ice, so how could you have gone ice-skating?'

'I might have known you would catch me out on that, Dad, so I must own up: it was a false story!'

CHAPTER 25

S o, one by one, they told their stories until it came to number fourteen, by which time they all knew who that was to be, but before Arnold could begin, Lucy apologised for interrupting, saying, 'I think I'd better get Mrs Craddock to take Anthony home, it's long past his bedtime!'

Once she had returned to the room, Arnold began: 'My story is true, and I experienced it some time ago. Because of it's lengthy content, I hope you don't mind if I stay sitting down to tell it to you.'

So settling himself down into his chair he began:

'When I was at the Choir School and reached the age of twelve, I was confirmed in the cathedral by the bishop. Leading up to that, I was asked to attend confirmation classes. These I did – with two other boys. The classes were held in the headmaster's house, which in those days was none other than Cowchester Hall.

The first time I went, I was shown into the dining room where we sat round a large table. On one side of the room was a very big fireplace, behind which, according to some of the older boys, a monk was bricked up alive for something he had done wrong a long time ago. Having heard many such stories about the cathedral in times gone by, I thought no more about it.

After leaving school, I started work in Beeley for the Electricity Supply Company, training to become an electrician. After five years I was given help in the form of a sixteen year-old boy called Terry, who was to learn the trade from me – just as I had done previously.

One Monday morning, the foreman said to me, 'I've got just the job for you!'

'Oh,' I said, (thinking, 'now what's coming?') and he said, 'Will you go round to the College to install some power points for Professor Rubin at Cowchester Hall?'

'Oh,' I said again! 'I know that place, I used to go for confirmation classes there.'

'Looking at the job sheet, I think you'll be there most of the week.'

So, gathering together the materials we needed, along with our tools, Terry and I set off on our bicycles for the Hall.

When we arrived, we walked up the garden path to the back door and rang the bell, which was answered by the housekeeper, Mrs Shaw. When I said why we had come, she said, 'Yes, I've been expecting you! Come in.'

We went down some steps into the kitchen while Mrs Shaw explained that the Professor was away in Cambridge and would not be back until Wednesday. Then she said, 'I know what is to be done so I can show you.'

'That's good,' I said. 'Is there anywhere we can put our tools?'

She answered, 'Yes, there's a room upstairs.'

Leading us up the backstairs to a door on the right at the end of the landing, she opened it and asked, 'Will this do?'

'Yes,' I said, 'it will do very nicely! Thank you.'

On seeing a lot of books on the floor, Terry started to pick them up and replace them in the bookcase under the window.

'It's no good you doing that!' said Mrs Shaw. 'They will all be back on the floor in the morning!"

Lucy gasped.

'Turning to her, I said, 'You don't mean this house is haunted?'

'Yes,' she answered."

At that, Lucy was beside herself and said, 'Oh, Michael!'

"So I said, 'You're having us on!'
'No, you ask the Professor when he comes back.'
I said, 'I will.'
So, putting the books to one side, we set to work.

About an hour later, Mrs Shaw called out, 'I've made some coffee, would you like some?'

'Yes, please!' I answered.

Joining her in the kitchen, we sat down at the table.

Over by the wall, a Siamese cat was asleep on a Windsor chair, and I remarked, 'He seems quite happy.'

She replied, 'Yes, that's his chair, he spends a lot of time there.'

Wanting to hear more about the haunting, I asked Mrs Shaw if she had ever seen anything unusual. She replied that she had, when her sister had been to stay.

So of course I wanted to know what had happened.

'Well,' said Mrs Shaw, putting down her cup. 'My sister was supposed to be coming for a week's holiday, but at breakfast on the second day she announced that she would be going straight back to London, and when I asked why she replied: 'I'm not staying in this house a moment longer: my things have been moved about in my room and last night I kept hearing strange noises.'

I told her there was nothing to worry about. It was an old house and there were bound to be noises, but no amount of pleading would persuade her to stay. I followed her up the backstairs to get her case and as she approached her room the door opened in front of her! She ran inside, grabbed her case and was gone!

Usually the cat lets us know when there's anything about, but on this occasion he was asleep downstairs. I have got used to the house now – as the professor has said many times, 'It's quite harmless!"

On the Wednesday, when Professor Rubin returned, I asked him if what Mrs Shaw had said was true and he replied that it was: 'We take no notice of it. We have a Siamese cat in the kitchen and he lets us know if there is anything about!'

Two days later, I went into the front hall to make the final connections to the meter. While squatting down by the front door, I suddenly heard the cat. Turning round to see what the noise was all about, I saw it standing halfway down the stairs with its back arched, fur bristling and its mouth open, making a cursing sound as if it was looking at something behind me.

I said, 'You silly old thing, you've seen me here all week. What's the matter with you?'

Then I turned and carried on with my work. It wasn't till later, when I'd had time to think about it, that I realised the cat was not alone in seeing what I was doing in the hall that morning!

I had occasion to revisit Cowchester Hall some time later, and whilst there I was offered a cup of tea. In conversation with the new occupant, I mentioned the fact that I had worked there a few years earlier, and was told the house was haunted. I gave an account of the cat incident and the books on the floor in the little room upstairs.

My host said, with a surprised look on his face, 'My little girl sleeps in that room at the top of the backstairs, and insists that sometimes at night, a man comes and sits on her bed and reads to her."

By now Lucy was quite distraught!

Arnold continued, ' Then he called his wife over, and I repeated what I had just said.'

Looking around, Arnold could see that he had everyone on the edge of their seats, especially Michael and Lucy who had both turned quite pale.

'-Well, that's my story and it's true, but I didn't want to worry anyone when I heard some of you were going to stay there with Uncle Harold!'

'Anthony kept telling us that a man came and sat on his bed at night and read to him, but we didn't believe him. We thought he had been dreaming – or was making it up!' said Lucy.

'What an extraordinary story!' exclaimed Lord Barnes. '-And to think my grandson should have had that experience!'

Lord Fortesque, who, like most of those present, had remained silent while Arnold was telling his story, said, 'I vote to accept Arnold's amazing account of what happened at Cowchester Hall as being the best we have listened to this evening, and with everyone's approval, I would like to nominate him to receive tonight's prize. Well done, Arnold!'

Everybody clapped.

The rest of the evening was spent discussing Arnold's remarkable account and the fact that Uncle Harold was still living there and had never seen anything unusual – or at least, had never spoken of it!

The following day, the guests said their goodbyes to Lord Barnes. Uncle Bertram said he hadn't enjoyed himself so much for years, and invited Lord Barnes, Michael and Lucy – not forgetting Anthony, for a long weekend at the farm, in the Spring. The invitation was readily accepted by Lord Barnes, and by Michael, who jokingly said he would not let his son go wandering off on his own again!

CHAPTER 26

When they arrived back at the Old Gatehouse, Lucy said to Michael, 'Do you know when Mr Parry is going to bring our Christmas tree?'

'This week, I hope,' replied Michael, 'but I will speak to him tomorrow to find out exactly when. I'm sure Mr Parry has things in hand already since the tree for the Manor went up early for the family weekend. I wonder what Father will be giving Anthony for Christmas this year?'

'You never can tell!' remarked Lucy. 'Your father's very fond of him. I notice Anthony will soon need a new pair of shoes, but I don't think he'd be very pleased if we gave them to him for Christmas!'

'It doesn't seem long since we bought him those shoes,' said Michael, dropping himself nicely in it!

'Well,' said Lucy, with a laugh, 'if you hadn't given him that football, those shoes would have lasted a lot longer! Changing the subject, has your father heard any more news about Mrs Druly, Michael?'

'I'll be seeing him in the morning, so I will ask him then, dear.'

'That poor woman is having quite a time of it – not knowing if she can marry or not. Everyone I have spoken to has said Matt seems like a nice sort of person, but you can never be certain, can you?'

'Well,' said Michael, drawing the conversation to a close, 'I had better see to things in the study.'

'And I must find young Master Anthony!' said Lucy. 'I hope he's not been getting under everyone's feet! Once Christmas is over, we really must do something about increasing the lesson time with his tutor. By the way, Michael, did you see that Mrs Warboys making up to your father?'

'Yes,' said Michael, 'I did. She seemed to be there whenever I tried to speak to him, and poor Lady Fortesque couldn't get a word in edgeways at dinner. Hilda Warboys hung on right to the end of the party weekend, hoping Father would ask her to stay one more night!'

Lucy said, 'Perish the thought, Michael! Those sort of people are only out for one thing.'

'I think my father is too clever to be taken in by the likes of her, my dear!'

The following morning, Michael went up to the Manor to see his father. When he arrived, William was still there.

'Hello William, how are things this morning?'

'Nice and quiet, thank you! I was just on my way to see Father.'

'That's where I'm heading!' said Michael.

As they entered the study, Lord Barnes said, 'I'm glad you are both here, I have something to tell you. I am going away for a few days' holiday with Hilda Warboys. After what you told me about your honeymoon in Scotland, William, I thought I would like to see it for myself. It so happens that Hilda Warboys knows of a very nice hotel where we can stay, so I must ask you both if you would keep an eye on things here whilst I am away?'

'How long will you be gone?' enquired Michael, diplomatically.

'I shall be away for five days – and by the look on your faces, I gather you don't approve!'

'Oh, it's nothing like that,' said Michael, hurriedly, '-only it has taken us by surprise!'

'Don't worry, I know what I am doing,' said Lord Barnes. 'I just thought it would be a chance to see another part of the country and I decided now would be as good a time as any to take a holiday there.'

'When were you thinking of leaving, Father?'

'This Friday. I have to chair a meeting on Thursday morning, so I shall just have time to get ready before I go.'

'Well, we both hope you have a lovely holiday, Father,' said William, finally managing to get a word in.

'Thank you, William.'

At that, the two brothers left the study, rather taken aback at what they had just been told.

When Michael returned home he said, 'Lucy, I've something to tell you!' Taking her by the hand, he pulled her into the study and shut the door. 'I don't want everyone to hear what I have to tell you – William and I have just seen my father and he told us he's going away for five days with that Hilda Warboys woman!'

'What!' exclaimed Lucy. 'The hussy! How has she managed to coerce your father into taking her away on a holiday with him?'

'I don't know,' said Michael. 'I just don't know! William was as surprised as I was, but Father did say not to worry and that he knew what he was doing.'

'Well,' said Lucy. 'I hope nothing comes of this. We can do without that sort of woman in our family!'

Friday soon arrived and it was time for Lord Barnes to leave for his holiday, Mr Parry taking him to the station to board the train for Scotland.

But Lord Barnes had other ideas…

When the train stopped at the next station, he got out and caught the ten fifty-five express to London, where he went straight to the War Office to enquire firstly about Joe Druly's death and secondly about the German Mrs Druly wanted to marry.

Not being satisfied with the answers he received, he left to investigate further, which took him out of the country.

Back at Caiston Manor, Mrs Brookes had a telephone call from a Mr Algernon Chapman, enquiring where Lord Barnes was staying in Scotland, but Mrs Brookes was always the soul of discretion and gave nothing away unless instructed by Lord Barnes to the contrary. Instead she said, 'I'm sorry, I cannot help you.'

The call bothered Mrs Brookes because she had never heard Lord Barnes mention this man before, so she made a note of his name and the time the call was received.

When Michael looked in at the Manor to enquire if all was well, Mrs Brookes told him of the telephone call and voiced her concern.

'I've never heard of the man before either,' said Michael. 'In any case, I wouldn't think my father would want to be bothered whilst on holiday.'

'And how is that son of yours, Mr Michael?' asked Mrs Brookes, changing the subject.

'As lively as ever, Mrs Brookes! He does love riding the pony his grandfather gave him, although he would like to have it stabled at home so he could ride it every day. But as I told him, ponies need to be looked after properly and at the farm it gets all the care and attention it requires. He wanted Lucy to take him to see his pony the other day hoping to get an extra ride, but Lucy's not keen to take him too often in case he picks up some of the farmworkers' bad words!'

'I'm glad to hear Miss Lucy's cold is better,' smiled Mrs Brookes.

'Yes, indeed! She seems to have got all her energy back now.'

'Well,' said Mrs Brookes, 'that's good news.'

After a week had elapsed, Lord Barnes was due to return home, but no-one knew exactly when, until Mrs Brookes received a telephone call from him late one evening, asking for Mr Parry to collect him from the station at twelve o'clock the next day. Knowing Mister Michael and Miss Lucy were concerned for Lord Barnes, she contacted the Old Gatehouse straight away.

The following afternoon, Michael received a message from his father, asking for the two brothers to see him as soon as possible since he had something to tell them both.

Lucy said, 'I wonder if he's going to tell you he has asked Mrs Warboys to marry him?'

'Oh, I hope not!' groaned Michael. 'I'd better go and find William so we can see what it's all about!'

CHAPTER 27

As the two brothers made their way towards the Manor, conversation was focussed on one topic only. Fearing the worst, they were both surprised and very relieved to hear from their father that he had not been on holiday after all. Instead he had been trying to find out answers to things which had been bothering him for some time regarding the Druly affair.

'Have you heard anymore from Mrs Druly, Father?'

'Yes, Michael. A letter arrived from her this morning and I have not long read it. Apparently she had a letter from a certain Bill Harper, who was a close friend of her late husband. In it, he said that during the war, he and five other men – including Joe, went on a raiding party one night to capture some German soldiers for interrogation. Unfortunately they ran into a German patrol who open-fired on them. Joe Druly was shot and left for dead. Bill Harper went back the next day to see if he could find his friend's body, but it was nowhere to be found, so Bill Harper assumed it had been removed for burial.'

'Poor woman!' said Michael. 'That must have brought everything back again.'

'Indeed,' said Lord Barnes. 'I was told she mourned her husband for weeks afterwards and now this letter will bring it all back – and that's not all,' he went on, 'apparently, when she showed the letter to Matt, his face went quite white and he hardly said another word to her all that day.'

'I suppose he must have seen some horrible things before he was captured,' said Michael.

'Yes, I should think so,' agreed Lord Barnes.

'By the way Father, Lucy asked me to thank you for letting us have a Christmas tree again this year.'

'It wouldn't be Christmas without a Christmas tree! Of course, I have mine in place already. What about you, William?'

'That's all right, Father, Caroline has already seen to that!'

There came a knock on the door.

'Come in,' said Lord Barnes. 'Oh, it's you, Mr Parry. Is anything wrong?'

'Yes, my lord. One of the Germans is missing. When it was time for roll-call there were only five instead of six present. The one who is missing is Matt, the man Mrs Druly is thinking of marrying. I have been round to her cottage but he's not there and Mrs Druly hasn't seen him for two days. The man in charge of the working party will report it when he gets back to camp. Mrs Druly is in shock and doesn't know what to think. her next door neighbour – as you know, that's Lucy's mother – is with her at the moment.'

'Well, Mr Parry, please keep me informed, and if there is anything I can do to help, please let me know.'

'Thank you, my lord.'

Turning to Michael, Lord Barnes said, 'I should think that poor woman is close to breaking point.'

'Would it help if Lucy went round to see her?' suggested Michael. 'She is good at being kind to people.'

'It would be splendid if she would.'

'Very well, Father, I will explain the position to Lucy and then she can pay Mrs Druly a visit. Look what the war has done to that woman: just as she thought she was making a new start in life after losing her husband, this happens.'

CHAPTER 28

The following morning, Lucy went to see Mrs Druly. She found her sitting at the kitchen table with her head in her hands. In front of her was a letter. When she saw Lucy, she asked her in, telling the children to put their coats on and play outside.

She started to read the letter to Lucy, but broke down sobbing, saying, 'I shall never see him again. He's gone back to Germany. He must have posted this before he went.' Still sobbing, she tried to continue reading the letter but gave up in despair.

'Would you like me to read it, Mrs Druly?'

Handing the letter to Lucy, she said, 'Do call me Betty. I'm sorry to be like this!'

'That's all right, Betty, I'll read it:

Dear Betty,

I am sorry not to have said goodbye, but when I read the letter you received from your husband's soldier friend, I realised I must make further enquiries about your husband. You see, during the war I was sent out with a raiding party to capture British soldiers for interrogation purposes. It so happened that this particular night, the British had also sent a raiding party to try to capture some of our men. On our way back we came across a wounded British soldier lying in the mud in no-man's land. One of our soldiers was just going to finish him off with his bayonet, when I stopped him by saying the wounded man might be able to give us some useful information. So we carried him back to our lines and searched him, but all we found was a small bloodstained book with a hole through it, containing words from the Gospel of St John.

From there he was taken to one of our field hospitals. What happened to him after that, I don't know, because two days later I was captured and sent to England, but I intend to find out.

Yours,
Matt.'

'Please Miss Lucy, don't think I have forgotten my husband. I shall always love him, but for the children's sake I thought I was doing right by having a man about the house and we got on so well.'

Suddenly there was an outburst from Betty's daughter, Janet, 'Mummy, Mummy, Mummy! Daddy's back!'

Mrs Druly jumped up and rushed to the door, then running down the garden path she flung her arms around the man standing there. Trembling all over and with tears of joy trickling down her face she cried, 'Joe, Joe, my dear Joe, you've come back to me!'

Lucy, feeling full of emotion, quietly left Betty and her daughter still clinging to Joe as they walked back into their home. As for three year-old Susan, she remained in the garden with a puzzled look on her face!

When Lucy arrived back home, Mrs Craddock noticed how pale she was and asked if she was feeling all right.

'Yes, thank you, Mrs Craddock, but I have had a bit of a shock. I've been to see Betty Druly and while I was there, her husband – whom we all thought was dead – returned home! You should have seen the joy on that woman's face as she flung her arms around him. I feel quite emotional, Mrs Craddock, but I must pull myself together and let his lordship know immediately.'

Going into the study, Lucy picked up the telephone and, with tears in her eyes, told his lordship all about her extraordinary visit to see Mrs Druly. When she had finished recounting the happenings, Lord Barnes said, 'I will get Mr Parry to visit them tomorrow to see if there is anything we can do to help should they need it. Meanwhile, I will contact the War Office to let them know of the dreadful mistake they have made in telling Mrs Druly that her husband was dead, and to suggest they offer her an apology for all the distress it has caused.'

Next morning, Mr Parry went to see his lordship.

'It's all over the village about Joe Druly coming back, my lord, but I don't know when he'll be starting work again, it all depends if he is well enough.'

Lord Barnes said, 'Will you go round and see Joe to find out how he is? He may not be well enough to start work straight away, but we must give him time, so tell him he can have his old job back again when he feels fit enough to start.'

'By the way, my lord, I was speaking to the person in charge of the German working party, and he told me that Matt had been found and will be required to explain his absence.'

'Did you have any idea this might happen, Mr Parry?'

'No, my lord, I didn't.'

'Well, Mr Parry, will you go now to see Joe and then report back to me on what you find?'

'Very good, my lord.'

'And after what you have just told me, I must make further enquiries regarding this mix-up and the reason for Matt's disappearance, although I have an idea what that's about.'

Just as Mr Parry was leaving the study, Mrs Brookes appeared, 'Just a reminder, my lord, that Master Anthony will be here in a few minutes for his morning ride.'

'Gracious, thank you for reminding me, Mrs Brookes. I have had a lot to deal with this morning. He's not here yet?'

'No, my lord.'

'Will you let me know when he arrives?'

After lunch Mr Parry returned to see his lordship.

'What news have you brought, Mr Parry?'

'Well, my lord, Joe Druly is certainly not ready to start work at his old job yet, but I think we could find him some light duties until he is fully recovered. It would give him something to live on, if that would meet your lordship's approval?'

'Yes, that would be most fitting.'

'One thing, my lord, while I was there his two little girls came into the room, and so I said, 'Isn't it nice to have your Daddy back again?' and the older girl said, 'Yes, it is,' going to sit on Joe's knee.

Then the younger one said, 'He's not my Daddy! My Daddy has gone away!'

'That's enough of that!' said Mrs Druly, sharply.

So I said, 'Well, your Daddy is back now.'

At that, Mrs Druly told both girls to go and play outside.

'What things children do come out with!' she said.

During all this, Joe had a puzzled look on his face – 'I don't think Mrs Druly has told her husband about Matt,' said Mr Parry.

'Well,' said his lordship, 'she will have to say something soon, otherwise he will hear it from someone else and we don't want that, do we? It could lead to all sorts of problems. I must ask Mrs Druly to come and see me as soon as possible.'

The next day, Lord Barnes travelled to London to learn more about the Druly case, which in turn would clarify why Matt had acted as he had.

CHAPTER 29

When Lord Barnes arrived back from London, he found a very worried-looking Mrs Brookes, who told him that George Fanshaw had called round earlier to see his lordship with the news that Mr and Mrs Druly had had a terrible disagreement during the night and that Joe had left home. '...And even more worrying is the fact that Mrs Druly was seen wading into the lake some hours later, apparently trying to drown herself.'

'Goodness me, Mrs Brookes! I must sit down. Is there any more?'

'Yes, my lord. Luckily, John Barton was on his way to work early this morning and happened to see Mrs Druly going into the water and was able to raise the alarm. Thankfully, they managed to get her out in time and immediately took her to the Infirmary.'

'Now, Mrs Brookes, can you find Mr Parry and ask him to see me as soon as possible?'

'Of course, my lord.'

At the Old Gatehouse, Lucy was talking to Michael about Mrs Druly and her two children when she heard Mrs Judd's raised voice, 'Oh, you naughty boy! Now look what you've done!'

Going into the kitchen, Lucy found Anthony with jam all over his hands, face and clothes, and a broken jampot on the floor. Seeing Lucy, Mrs Judd said, 'He has been watching me fill the pastry cases with strawberry jam, and as soon as my back was turned, he stuck his hand in the jam pot – and now look!'

'That's all right, Mrs Judd, I'll see to him. -You are a naughty boy to get jam all over yourself! Just look at you!'

'-But I was trying to get the strawberry, Mummy!'

'I must get you out of those messy clothes. I've a good mind not to let you go riding today at your grandfather's.'

'But I didn't mean to be naughty, Mummy!' whimpered Anthony.

It wasn't long before Mr Parry arrived to see his lordship.

'Have you heard about the Drulys, my lord?'

'Yes, Mr Parry. Mrs Brookes has told me. Now, would you go round to Joe's house and find out what is happening there, particularly regarding the children – who is looking after them? And then, will you go to the Infirmary to see how Mrs Druly is, and report back to me?'

Mr Parry lost no time in carrying out his lordship's wishes, returning a short time later to report his findings.

'Come in, Mr Parry. What news?'

'Well, my lord, when I arrived at the Druly's house there was no one there. I saw this letter on the table so I brought it back for you to see.'

Taking the letter from Mr Parry, Lord Barnes began to read:

'Betty,

I thought you loved me, but it seems I was wrong.

With me out of the way, you would rather have a blinking German. I thought I knew you better.

I can't live here with you after that. I am going away and you will never see me again.

Go marry your German,
Goodbye.'

Looking up from the letter in his hand, Lord Barnes sighed, 'This is just what I didn't want to happen. Now – what about the children, Mr Parry?'

'Mrs Fanshaw, who, as you know, lives next door, is looking after them for the time being.'

'That's good,' said his lordship. 'Now, what about Mrs Druly?'

'Well, my lord, they have made her comfortable at the Infirmary, but she seems to have lost her memory.'

'I'm not surprised,' remarked his lordship. 'Poor woman!' Sitting back in his chair he said, 'Well, Mr Parry, what do we do now? If only I could have explained the situation to Joe it might have averted all this trouble. I wonder if the letter from Joe Druly's army friend might be anywhere in the cottage, because if I contacted him he might be able to find Joe and bring him back home.'

'Shall I go and have another look in the Druly's house, my lord?'

'Yes, Mr Parry, but ask Mrs Fanshaw and the older daughter to go in with you. They may be able to find it for you. If anyone asks what you are doing there, just say I asked you to investigate where Bill Harper's letter, bearing his address, might be.'

'Very good, my lord!'

So Mr Parry went back once more, and with the help of Mrs Fanshaw and Janet, was able to find the letter and bring it back to his lordship.

Lord Barnes lost no time in writing, and after a few days had passed, Mrs Brookes announced, 'There's a Mr William Harper here to see you, my lord.'

170

'Show him in, Mrs Brookes… Come in and sit down, Mr Harper. What I have to tell you may take a little while.'

When his lordship had finished, Bill Harper said, 'I am delighted Joe is alive. I know he can be a bit quick-tempered at times, but he should have listened to his wife and not gone off like that. I will go now, and see if I can find him. When we were in the trenches he often spoke of a place he seemed fond of before the war – if only I could remember where that was. When it comes to mind, I will start looking there and when I find him I will bring him back to you, my lord.'

'Perhaps by seeing her husband again it may help Mrs Druly regain her memory and get better. Now I must contact my daughter-in-law to ask her to visit her mother, who lives next door to the Drulys, to see how she is managing looking after the two girls.'

Leaving his lordship, Bill Harper went on his way, intent on finding his soldier friend.

Picking up the telephone, Lord Barnes spoke to Lucy.

When he had finished, Mr Parry was waiting to see him to say that Mrs Druly was a little better and that she was beginning to remember things again.

'That's encouraging news, Mr Parry.'

'Yes, my lord.'

'Now all we have to do is wait for Bill Harper to find Joe.'

'By the way, my lord, the person in charge of the German workers, told me this morning that we can keep them a little longer if we like.'

'Oh, that is good news, Mr Parry. We'll be coming up to a busy time on the land in the New Year and will need all the help we can get.'

'Well, my lord, if there is nothing else, I will be on my way.'

Down at the Old Gatehouse, Lucy said to Mrs Craddock, 'I have to go and see how my mother is getting on with the two Druly girls. She told me yesterday that they are good, well-behaved children, but that they are missing their mother and father. I do hope Betty gets her memory back soon!'

'So do I, Miss Lucy. What that poor woman has had to put up with! Let's hope she is soon back home again.'

'Yes, his lordship told me this morning that he has asked Joe Druly's soldier friend to help find Joe. Now, I must be off. I'm sure Anthony will be a good boy. He's in the washhouse playing with his boat and I left Agnes to keep an eye on him.'

When Lucy arrived at her parent's cottage, she found her mother reading a story to the two children. On seeing Lucy, she stopped – much to the disappointment of the girls who were enjoying being read to.

'I'm sure my mother will finish reading the story when I've gone, but I would like to speak to her first, so would you both go and play with your toys for a few minutes? Here are some sweets for you both, we won't be long!'

CHAPTER 30

It was early in the New Year before Lord Barnes heard
from Bill Harper, who said he had found Joe Druly
living rough and begging for food.

'As soon as he saw me he broke down in tears and
said, 'What a fool I have been!' and vowed to make
amends. I will be bringing him back tomorrow morning,
my lord.'

Lord Barnes immediately asked Lucy to tell her mother
that Joe would be returning home the next day to see his
children, and hopefully, to stay.

About eleven o'clock the next morning, Mrs Brookes knocked on the study door and announced that Mr Harper and Mr Druly were there to see his lordship.

'Ask them to come in, Mrs Brookes.'

Then Lord Barnes welcomed both men and thanked them for coming to see him. He listened intently to Joe's account of his near-fatal injury and the mystery surrounding how he eventually found himself in a German hospital. Then he thanked Bill Harper for finding Joe and rewarded him for his trouble. After saying goodbye to his friend and promising to keep in touch, Bill Harper left the room.

'Now,' said Lord Barnes, 'I'm not going to lecture you, Joe, because I know you've had a rough time, but I must explain how things happened right from the start...'

A little later, Lord Barnes concluded by saying, 'Just cast your mind back to those horrible times. What would you have done if you had come across a badly injured German? Would you have stopped your comrades from sticking their bayonets into him? Just think, you owe your life to this man, so I will say no more, only to applaud you for coming back. Your wife loves you and it's you she needs to get her well again, and your two lovely children need their father. I have asked Mr Parry to find you light duties for the time being and when you are well enough you can have your old job back.'

'Thank you, my lord, for all that you have done for me and my family, and for explaining how it all came about.

I must go to my wife and ask for her forgiveness and then I'll go and find my two daughters.'

'They will be overjoyed to see you.'

And so, after leaving the Manor, Joe Druly went to the Infirmary to see his wife, a visit which he found extremely distressing, knowing that it was largely his fault she was there. Feeling full of remorse and vowing to help her get better, he left for home, determined never to leave his family again.

It took several weeks for Betty Druly to recover, but recover she did, and eventually the day came for her to return to her husband and little girls – much to the delight of everyone.

CHAPTER 31

I t was late Spring when Michael went to see his father to report on the slow progress being made with the building of the new cottages.

'The way things are going, I doubt they will get the roofs on before Christmas!'

'Well, Michael, we will just have to hope that the weather is kind. Meantime, I will have a word with Mr Mord, the builder, to see if he can hurry the job along. By the way, I had a letter this morning from Bertram Fortesque. Mary is getting married in the summer and he has invited us all to the wedding.'

'Oh, I must tell Lucy, she will be pleased. They made us very welcome when we stayed there and I know Anthony will want Peter to give him another ride on the pony.'

'Yes, he will like that!' said Lord Barnes. 'I do hope it isn't during the two weeks I have to be in London. Still, you could all go.'

When Michael arrived home he told Lucy the news about the wedding, mentioning that his father might not be able to join them. 'I think he said that since William and Caroline live nearer, they might be able to travel on the morning of the wedding – which, I understand, isn't until the afternoon. When my father has been in touch with Uncle Bertram, we'll know more. I don't think we ought to say anything to Anthony until then.'

The telephone rang. 'I'd better go and answer it,' sighed Michael. Leaving Lucy, he made his way to the study and on picking up the receiver, heard William's voice.

'Hello, Michael! It's William here! Caroline and I have some good news to tell you. Can we come to see you both tomorrow morning?'

'Of course you can!' replied Michael, 'but can't you tell me now?'

'No, Michael. I would rather bring Caroline over to see you both.'

'Very well,' said Michael, 'until then, goodbye!'

Putting the receiver down, Michael went back to Lucy. 'Who was that?' she asked.

'It was William. He and Caroline want to come over in the morning to see us both. They have some good news to tell us – and I wonder what that good news is?'

'I think I can guess!' said Lucy, 'but we must wait and see!'

'Where's Anthony?' asked Michael.

'He's all right, he's playing with his boat in the washhouse.'

Michael went to find him but couldn't see his son anywhere.

'Where's Anthony, Agnes?'

'He went outside to empty the water out of his boat, Mister Michael. Shall I go and get him for you?'

'No, I'll go,' replied Michael.

As he looked around the kitchen garden, his son was nowhere to be seen. Finally he spotted him, trying to lift the latch on the gate which led on to the lakeside.

'Anthony! Come here at once! What do you think you are doing?'

'I want to sail my boat on the lake, Daddy, but I can't open the gate!'

'Now Anthony, you must not go down to the lake by yourself, it's very deep and very dangerous. Before we lived here, a little girl died by falling into the water. If you want to sail your boat on the lake you must ask me or your mother to be with you, just in case you fall in and need rescuing. Do you understand, Anthony?'

'Yes, Daddy.'

'Now, Anthony, one more thing: if you sail your boat on the lake without a string attached to it, the boat will sail away across the lake and you will lose it, and we wouldn't want that to happen, would we?'

'No, Daddy.'

'Well, then – you know what you must do: ask your mother or me to be with you when you want to sail your boat on the lake and we will tie a piece of string to it so you can pull it back when you've finished playing with it.'

Going back into the washhouse, he told Anthony to stay there. 'Agnes, please keep a close eye on him. He must not go outside.'

'Very good, Mister Michael.'

Next morning, William and Caroline arrived to see Michael and Lucy. William said, 'Caroline has some news to tell you!'

'Yes,' replied Caroline, 'I am expecting a baby towards the end of the year and we wanted you to be the first to know!'

'Congratulations to you both! We are very pleased for you.' Turning to Lucy, Michael said, 'I will be an Uncle!'

'-And I will be an Aunt!' exclaimed Lucy. 'You must look after yourself Caroline. Your parents will be over the moon – I wonder what Uncle Bertram will say when you tell him!'

'William and I are going to the farm on the weekend to see him!' smiled Caroline, 'and I'm going to help Mary choose some clothes for her honeymoon.'

Lucy said, 'Remember us to them when you're there.'

'I will,' replied Caroline.

CHAPTER 32

The following morning, Michael had a telephone call from his father, to say that he had been in touch with Uncle Bertram regarding Mary's wedding. He had given his apologies for being unable to attend, but was pleased to say that Michael and family would be delighted to go, therefore Michael could expect to receive an invitation in a day or two.

Michael said how sorry he was that his father would not be joining them as they had had such a lovely time on their previous visit.

'Yes,' said Lord Barnes. 'They are a very nice family and quite knowledgeable on farming matters. I would like to have another chat with Bertram sometime about his methods of crop rotation – I found it most interesting.'

'I've yet to see finer fields of wheat than he had when I was there,' said Michael. 'Mind you, he has very different soil to work with than we do around here.'

'Well, I hope you all have a very happy time!'

'Thank you, Father.'

Just then, Lucy came into the study. 'Who was that, Michael?'

'It was my father, regarding Mary's wedding…' and after telling Lucy all about the conversation, he said, 'I am disappointed my father can't come, but perhaps he can visit the farm another time.'

'I do hope so,' replied Lucy.

That weekend, William and Caroline went to stay with Uncle Bertram and family, and while they were there Mary said to Caroline, 'I am so glad you're willing to help me with what I should pack for my honeymoon.'

'It will be fun!' replied Caroline, 'but what you take with you depends on where you are going.'

'Rupert has seen a very nice hotel advertised and it's in Devon, by the sea, so we thought we would stay there.'

'That sounds lovely,' replied Caroline.

'You haven't met Rupert yet, have you? He will be coming to see us this evening. His father keeps the local shop and Post Office here in Wentley village – that's where Rupert works. He sometimes drives the van, delivering goods from the shop to the more out-of-the-way farms as well.'

'Yes,' interrupted Peter, who had been listening to what Mary had been saying, 'but we don't mention his surname as it makes some people laugh!'

'Well, whatever is it then?' asked William, intrigued.

Mary, looking a little embarrassed, said, 'His name is Rupert Shortass!'

William turned away, trying not to laugh, but Caroline could not contain herself!

Mary said, 'Trust you to bring that up right now, Peter!'

Uncle Bertram, who had been quiet until now, chuckled, 'If we want anything from the local shop we usually say, 'Go and see if Harry sells it!' -that's Rupert's father's name. Rupert's a very nice young man.'

'Yes, I'm sure he is,' said Caroline, 'otherwise Mary wouldn't be marrying him!'

'How is young Anthony getting on?' enquired Uncle Bertram, who was wanting to change the subject.

'Full of mischief!' replied William. 'I think Michael and Lucy have got their hands full with him at the moment – he gets into all sorts of trouble! Michael bought him a football, much to Lucy's dismay, and his favourite game seems to be kicking it at the kitchen staff! He saw Mrs Judd bending down to pick something up and he kicked the ball, hitting her fair and square on the backside, nearly knocking her over, for which he was sent upstairs to his bedroom!'

'What else has he been doing?' enquired Peter, who was enjoying listening to all this and hoping for more stories of Anthony's activities!

'Oh, his grandfather gave him a pony, which he loves to ride when Michael or Lucy can spare the time to take him. So now they have something to use when Anthony misbehaves: by saying he can't go riding that week, they are hoping he will start to behave himself!'

'Well,' said Mary, 'Rupert and I were wondering if Anthony would be a page boy at our wedding.'

'Are you sure he will behave himself?' remarked William.

'I will have to ask Lucy first to see what she thinks,' said Mary. 'There's Rupert's young brother who is going to be the other page boy.'

'I shall look forward to the wedding for more than one reason then!' said William, with a broad grin on his face.

'I hope we have weather like this for our wedding. It was hot yesterday and it looks as if it might be the same again today,' said Mary.

'Although I will be glad when the cooler weather comes!' remarked Aunt Annie. 'It's a job to keep the milk and butter from going off, despite the dairy being quite cold most of the time as it's on the North side of the house and partly shaded by trees. I expect we will have thunderstorms when this weather breaks – just as long as it doesn't rain for the wedding!'

'No, we don't want that!' exclaimed Caroline.

The next day, William suggested to Caroline that they walked down to the farm after they had finished their breakfast.

Caroline said, 'Well, dear, Mary has asked me to help her with her going-away things this morning. You don't mind, do you?'

'No,' said William, 'but I think I will have a wander down to the farm anyway.'

'You won't find anyone there, only George Halfsharp!' interrupted Aunt Annie. 'My husband and Peter are going to market to buy another cow and won't be back until late this afternoon.'

'Never mind,' said William, 'the walk will do me good!'

When he arrived at the farm, he found George Halfsharp in one of the stables, scattering straw about for the horses to lie on, and every now and then, he mopped his forehead with a large red handkerchief.

'Hello, George!'

'Morning, Mister William! Isn't it hot?'

'Yes,' said William, 'it looks like another scorcher!'

'The Master and Peter have gone to buy another cow at market.'

'So they have left you in charge while they're away?'

'That's right!' said George. 'How is young Master Anthony getting on? I bet the next time he comes here, he'll keep away from the geese! That old gander goes for me when I go to feed them in the morning, but as soon as I throw the corn down, he thinks better of it and stops to feed! Well, Mister William, I must get on.'

Leaving George, William went round the farm keeping an eye open for the geese, as he himself didn't fancy an encounter with the gander! He was surprised to hear the chickens making a squawking noise as if something was after them. Going over to investigate, he saw a fox come darting out of the hen-house with a chicken in it's mouth and then making off across the field. William went back to tell George Halfsharp, but stopped short when he saw George coming towards him with a shotgun!

'That fox has just made off with one of the hens, George!'

'I'll give him both barrels from this if he comes back!' said George, waving the gun.

'I didn't think foxes came out in the daytime,' said William.

'I expect he's got a family. They get very daring when there are several mouths to feed.'

'Do you think he'll come back again?'

'Quite probably,' replied George.

'Would you like me to stay here and watch? I have nothing special on at the moment,' said William.

'You will have to hide in here to look out for it then. Can you shoot, Mister William?'

'Yes, I can.'

'Well, take this, and if he comes back I hope you get it!'

William sat down and waited. He could see the hen-house from where he was sitting and wondered what Uncle Bertram would say if he managed to shoot the fox!

But it didn't reappear. So after returning the gun to George, he made his way back to the house to find Caroline and Mary.

CHAPTER 33

After lunch, Mary said to William, 'Would you like to see a picture of the man I'm going to marry?'

'Yes, please,' replied William.

Mary picked up a photo album and sat down beside him.

Caroline sat on the other side. As they looked at the pictures of Rupert and Mary, Aunt Annie came into the room and quipped, 'A thorn between two roses!' Then laughed, 'That makes a lovely picture – you three sitting there!'

Hardly had she said that, when George Halfsharp came panting into the farmhouse shouting, 'Get the fire brigade – the haystack's on fire!'

William jumped up and ran to the door. Aunt Annie rushed to the telephone to make the call. Caroline and Mary followed William who was already on his way to the farm to see what he could do. As it happened, the haystack was well away from the farm buildings and on one side of the farmyard, over by the hedge which was already partly burnt away by the intense heat of the fire.

After a few minutes, George Halfsharp arrived, still out of breath after his mad dash to raise the alarm.

'I've moved the animals out of the buildings nearest the fire, but we may have to shift the three calves from their shed,' spluttered George.

'All right,' said William. '-Ah! I think I can hear the fire brigade coming!'

The first thing they asked was, 'Are all the animals out of the buildings?'

'All except three calves,' replied George.

'Well, get them out – just in case,' advised the fireman.

It wasn't long before water was being sprayed on the haystack, which by now was well alight. George said, 'Whatever will the master say when he gets back?'

William replied, 'It wasn't your fault, George, it was the weather – haystacks are notorious for catching fire when it's hot like this. The heat builds up in the middle of the stack and that's what causes the fire. I expect

Uncle Bertram has got ways of checking it from time to time?'

'Yes,' said George. 'I've often seen the master push a long iron rod with a hook at the end into the haystack, so he can test how hot it is in the middle when he pulls it out. You would be surprised how hot it gets! Sometimes the stack has to be opened up to let the heat out and stop it from catching fire.'

Mary said to Caroline, as they stood watching, 'We can't do any good here. Dad won't be very pleased because he's just lost the hay which he had earmarked for the animals' winter feed. Now he'll have to start looking round to buy hay to replace this lot! As if Dad hasn't got enough on his plate at the moment! Oh, do let's go back home now.'

When they arrived back, Aunt Annie wanted to know all that had happened and how bad things were at the farm.

Mary said, 'I'm afraid the haystack has gone, but luckily none of the buildings have been affected and all the animals are safe.'

'Oh, I am pleased about that – what a relief!' sighed Aunt Annie.

William stayed at the farm for the rest of the afternoon. When the fire was under control, he said to George, 'I expect my wife and Miss Mary will have told Aunt Annie what has happened. She must have been very worried. I think I'd better be off now, but I may be back when Uncle Bertram returns.'

It was over an hour before Uncle Bertram and Peter put in an appearance. By the time they had arrived at the farm, the firemen had put out all the flames and were dousing down what was left of the hay.

'If only we hadn't gone to buy that cow, Peter, I might have prevented this. Checking the hay during this hot weather was one of my jobs. I would normally have done it this morning, but since we were going to market and needed to get away in good time, I thought it would be all right for one more day. I must have a word with the firemen to see when it is safe to move the animals back to their sheds.'

Peter said to George Halfsharp, 'You did well to get the animals out of the buildings and away from the fire, George. Losing the haystack is bad enough, but to have lost the animals as well would have been a catastrophe! Now we just have to wait until they say we can get this mess cleared up.'

It was nearly dark when Uncle Bertram and Peter returned to the house. Aunt Annie said to her husband, 'Come and sit down and I will get you something nice to eat and drink.'

'I'm not very hungry, Mother. I could do with a drink though. It's been quite a day, hasn't it? Still, it's no good crying over spilt milk – I will just have to look round to see where I can buy hay for the winter.'

Arnold, who had arrived home earlier, said, 'When I called in at Harry's, they told me about the fire. That will be the talk of the village for the next few days! Still, that's a change from hearing about old Aggie Cowslip having too much to drink at the Red Lion and spending the night asleep on the village green!' Then, turning to William, he added, 'Some of the local boys played a joke on her and when she was asleep, they tied a rope around her, fastening her to the seat, so when she came to she couldn't get up! She'll never hear the last of that!'

'My word!' exclaimed William, who was enjoying listening to Arnold, 'You do see life here!'

'Yes, there's never a dull moment in this village!' said Peter, laughing.

'It's a pity we have to go home tomorrow, Caroline, I'm quite enjoying being here -apart from the fire. You seem to have a lot of fun in this village!'

'We do,' said Peter, '-what about the time when that carpet salesman…'

'That's enough of that, Peter! I'm sure William and Caroline don't want to hear about that!' interrupted Aunt Annie.

'Oh – how disappointing!' said William, with a broad grin on his face.

'Perhaps I will tell you the next time you come!' replied Peter, laughing.

The following morning, William and Caroline said their farewells and returned home to Willow Tree Lodge.

The day after their return, William said to Caroline, 'I'd better go to see my father and brother to find out how things are on the Estate and tell them about the fire on Uncle Bertram's farm.'

Caroline said, 'Perhaps your father might be able to help my uncle in replacing the hay he lost?'

'That's just what I was thinking!' replied William. 'I'm sure he would be only too willing – we had a good crop of hay on the Estate this year, so perhaps we would be able to let Uncle Bertram have some. I'll suggest that to my father and to Michael when I see them.'

When William arrived at the Manor, he found his father in conversation with Mr Parry.

'Come in, my boy!' said Lord Barnes. 'Have you had a good time at your Uncle Bertram's?'

'Yes, thank you, Father, but while we were there the haystack caught fire and the fire brigade were called out. Now Uncle Bertram has lost all his hay and has got to buy some in for the animals before the winter comes.'

'I'm sorry to hear that. What is our state of hay at the moment, Mr Parry?'

'Well, my lord, we have been fortunate this year – in fact we have more hay than we will need. That was one thing I wanted to speak to you about.'

'Then let me know what we can spare, Mr Parry, and I will contact Bertram Fortesque to tell him we can help.'

'Very well, my lord. If that's all, I'll be on my way.'

'Thank you, Father. I'm sure Uncle Bertram will be grateful for your help. They are having to cart all the ash from the fire on to the land to be ploughed in, and a damaged hedge will also have to be repaired. It's surprising what there is to do after a fire.'

'Yes, my boy, I know only too well!'

CHAPTER 34

After leaving his lordship, William went to see Michael. When he arrived, he found Lucy telling Anthony off for being rude to Mrs Judd.

'What's this young rascal been up to now, Lucy?'

'It's that football again, William! Anthony kicked it into the kitchen, so Mrs Judd has taken it and hidden it away so Anthony can't play with it, and I think he said something rude to her as a result!'

William laughed, 'He seems to have it in for Mrs Judd!'

'Well,' said Lucy. 'None of us are getting any younger

and I don't think Mrs Judd wants to have a fall at her time of life!'

'I don't blame her for being careful,' said William. 'Now, where's that husband of yours?'

'Michael has gone to see Nigel at the farm. I'm expecting him back soon. Why don't you stop and have a drink with us -if you have time?'

'Thank you, Lucy, I will.' Turning to Anthony, he said, 'So, young man, how's that pony of yours? I expect you've been riding up at the Manor with your grandfather?'

Before Anthony could answer, Lucy cut in, 'Because he was rude to Mrs Judd, we said he could not go riding this week.'

'Well,' said William, 'you have a lot of nice things to look forward to, Anthony, but you must be kind to people and then they will be kind to you – it works both ways! It's Mrs Judd who makes you those little pastry men with currants in. I hear you like them, so if you are unkind to her, she won't want to make them for you any more.'

On hearing that, Anthony went straight into the kitchen and said, 'Sorry!' to Mrs Judd and, 'Please may I have my ball back?'

Mrs Judd looked at Anthony and was about to tell him off, when her feelings got the better of her and she said, 'I forgive you this time, but try to be a good boy and not to play with it in the kitchen!'

'Thank you, Mrs Judd!'

Feeling very pleased with himself for getting his ball back, Anthony went to find his Uncle William, who was still talking to his mother. When they saw Anthony, they stopped talking and William remarked, 'I see you've got your ball back, Anthony! How did you manage that?'

'I told Mrs Judd I was sorry.'

'Good boy,' said his mother, '- now, how would you like to go to the fair next weekend?'

Anthony's face lit up. 'Yes, please, Mummy!'

William butted in adding, 'You will have to be a good boy for the whole of this week though. Do you think you can do that?'

'I think that might be asking a lot,' said Lucy, 'but we shall see!'

Just then, Michael came in, 'Oh, hello, William. Did you want to see me?'

'Well, all three of you really! There's a fair coming next weekend and I was reminding Lucy about it. I wondered if the four of us could go on Saturday?'

'That will be nice,' said Michael. 'But what about Caroline?'

'Caroline's not keen on fairs and thought she would spend the afternoon with her mother if you decided you'd like to go too.'

'I'll get some rock for Father!'

'I didn't know he liked rock!' exclaimed William.

'Yes! He bought some when he and I went on holiday before I was married, so now Lucy and I always buy him some whenever we visit the fair. He's got a sweet tooth where rock is concerned! If you like, William, you can be the one to give it to him this time – and watch his reaction when he looks inside the bag!'

'I shall look forward to that!' chuckled William.

As the days went by, Anthony was getting more and more excited about going to the fair. Finally, Saturday arrived and Michael said, 'I must telephone my father to remind him where we will be today in case he forgets and wants help with the quarterly returns on the Estate – they're due this week.'

After talking to his father, Michael said, 'That's settled – I'm going to help him on Monday.' Just as he had finished talking to Lucy, William put in an appearance, 'Are we all ready, then?'

'Yes,' said Michael, 'let's go!' and the four of them left straight away.

The fair was in full swing when they arrived. Lucy said, 'I must take Anthony for a ride on the roundabout, that's the thing he's been looking forward to all this week!'

Michael turned to his brother, 'William, shall we try to win a coconut?'

'That's a good idea!' replied William, so off they went.

As Lucy walked with Anthony to the children's roundabout, she was unaware that someone was watching her, following her every move as she put Anthony on one of the little horses. As she stood there, watching Anthony go round and round, she was approached by Mrs Druly who said, 'My Susan is having a ride on here as well – it's lovely for children, isn't it? Joe has taken Janet on the Gallopers.'

After a while engrossed in conversation, Lucy became aware that the roundabout had stopped and she immediately looked round for Anthony, but he was nowhere to be seen. Lucy said to Betty, who had just collected Susan, 'Have you seen Anthony? I can't find him!'

Having another look, once more without success, Lucy began to panic and ran to find Michael and William, who, when they heard that Anthony was missing, started to make enquiries at some of the stalls to see if anyone had seen a small boy, dressed in a blue jacket, walking about on his own. But no one had.

They carried out a thorough search of the fairground, then Lucy, who by now was beside herself with worry, said, 'We must get in touch with the local police station.'

Having done that, Lord Barnes was informed, and on hearing that his grandson was missing, lost no time in contacting his friend, the Police Inspector.

After speaking to several more people at the fairground, one stallholder thought he remembered a small boy, dressed in a blue jacket, walking past, holding the hand of a man in a grey raincoat, so once the police arrived, a description of this man was circulated and people were asked to keep a sharp look out and to report any sighting straight away.

A little later, at the Old Gatehouse, Mrs Craddock was having a hard time trying to console Lucy, who by now had returned home and was blaming herself for not being more careful in keeping an eye on what was happening.

'Who is this man and what does he want with my son?' she repeated over and over again. Whilst at Caiston Manor, Lord Barnes was telling the Police Inspector all he knew about Anthony's disappearance.

'Please do all you can to find my grandson,' he urged.

At this point, and seeing his lordship in an unusually distressed state, the Inspector said, 'Have no fear, my lord. I will do all in my power to find your grandson, but I must get back now in order to organise a thorough search of the area.'

'Very well,' said his lordship, and at that, the Inspector departed. Lord Barnes immediately picked up the telephone and spoke to Michael, wanting to know if there was any further news.

'No, Father. We haven't heard any more.'

'Will you see that all the buildings on the Estate are checked, Michael, just to make sure that Anthony hasn't been hidden there. I must stay here by the telephone in case the Inspector should call me.'

'I understand, Father. William is at the farm already making a thorough search and I will let you know if we have anything to report. I'm having a difficult time here with Lucy. She's distraught for not having been more vigilant.'

'Very well,' said Lord Barnes, 'tell her everything is being done to find Anthony and I hope and pray it won't be long before we have news of him.'

As time passed and it began to get dark, fears for the boy's safety mounted, and just before eleven o'clock that night, the Inspector called to see Lord Barnes, with the news that Anthony was nowhere to be seen. He added that the police would continue their search throughout the night and as soon as there was any news, his lordship would be the first to know.

The family spent a sleepless night, worrying for the boy's safety until just before seven o'clock, when Mrs Brookes answered the front door to the Inspector, who asked to see his lordship.

Lord Barnes was down the stairs in an instant, 'Any news, Inspector?'

'Yes, my lord. Your grandson has been found safe and well and none the worse for his adventure. He will be returned later on this morning. That is all I can say at this time, but I will call again to give a full report on everything that has happened when I am in possession of all the facts.'

Lord Barnes was overjoyed, and straightway telephoned Michael to tell him the good news that Anthony was safe and well, and would be arriving home later that morning. He was determined to be there for Anthony's return, and made his way to the Old Gatehouse immediately after breakfast where he found Lucy, Michael and William in buoyant mood, and hugs of relief were exchanged.

Then, shortly after ten o'clock, a police car drew up at the gate. The driver got out of the car, walked round and opened the door for young Anthony, who ran straight into his mother's arms.

He was soon surrounded by family and staff, all wishing him well, and feeling very relieved to have him back – even Mrs Judd!

True to his word, the Inspector called later that morning to see them all at the Old Gatehouse.

'Late last night, one of the porters at the railway station happened to see a man and boy answering the description given, getting on the train to London. He reported it to the local police, who in turn passed the information on to us. As the train was non-stop to London, I contacted the London police, who made sure they were there, ready to apprehend the man when he tried to leave the railway station.'

'Who was that man?' demanded Lord Barnes.

'It's our old friend, Felix!'

'But I thought he was in prison!' replied Lord Barnes.

'Yes, he was, but he escaped two weeks ago.'

'Well,' said Lord Barnes, 'this man has become a menace to our family and I hope that he will be put away for a very long time.'

'I will make certain all the facts about this man are known, my lord,' said the Inspector.

Michael said, 'It's a good thing the porter was so prompt in reporting this, we've been nearly out of our minds with worry.'

'The railway stations are among the first places we notify in a case like this,' replied the Inspector.

'I can't thank you enough, for all the trouble you have taken,' said Lord Barnes, shaking the Inspector warmly by the hand.

When the Inspector had gone, Michael said to Anthony, who was in excellent spirits, 'What happened to you at the fair?'

But all Anthony could talk about was his ride in the police car and how fast they went!

After a while, William turned to his father and said, 'With all that has happened, I almost forgot – I have something for you!' Handing over a paper bag, he added, 'I didn't know you had a sweet tooth!'

Lord Barnes, being a bit surprised at this, took the bag and on looking inside, grinned broadly and said, 'You have been talking to Michael!' -at which everyone laughed!

CHAPTER 35

It was the week of Mary's wedding, and the vicar, the Reverend Marmaduke Clutterbug, had suggested they have a rehearsal the day before, which meant Michael, Lucy and Anthony would have to stay overnight somewhere.

They decided to follow up Uncle Bertram's suggestion that they try 'The Cat and Fiddle' in Wentley village.

The landlord said he had just one double room left and that it was large enough to accommodate a small bed for Anthony. He added that they would be full that night however, as they were hosting a Stag Night for one of the village lads who was getting married the next day.

When Michael told Lucy, she said, 'Well, we know who that is and it sounds as if we're in for a lively time then! I wonder where William and Caroline will be staying?'

'William hasn't said anything,' replied Michael. 'Perhaps they will be sleeping in the attic room – along with the swallows – at Uncle Bertram's! I'll ask him later today. I must also make sure Father remembers we're away for two nights and not just one, because he goes away to London this week, so it's important for Mr Parry to be around in everyone's absence.'

'Yes, and I must remember to tell Mrs Craddock that we'll be away too.'

Friday morning came, and Michael, Lucy and Anthony set off on their journey to Wentley village. On arrival, they made their way to 'The Cat and Fiddle' which was already busy serving drinks and Ploughman's lunches, these being helped down by a rendition of a song about a drunken sailor, sung by a man with a raucous voice and accompanied by a sprightly grey-haired lady who was pounding a honky-tonk piano.

When they had deposited their cases in their room, Michael said, 'Shall we go to Aunt Annie's now to find out what time we'll be needed in the church this afternoon?'

'What about something to eat first?' suggested Lucy.

'I'm hungry too, but I think we ought to get to the farmhouse to let them know we're here.'

The moment they walked through the door, Aunt Annie said, 'You have come just right to join us for lunch. Sit down and make yourselves comfortable. What's it like at 'The Cat and Fiddle' this morning?'

'Quite busy and very noisy!' said Michael.

'Oh!' said Mary. 'I've heard there's a lady who plays the piano sometimes.'

'Yes,' said Michael. 'She was letting rip when we arrived, and a man with a very loud and raucous voice was trying to outdo her in a song about a sailor!'

'I hear it gets even more rowdy on a Saturday night!' remarked Aunt Annie.

'That should be interesting!' said Michael.

'When are William and Caroline arriving?' enquired Lucy.

'They will be here this afternoon in time for the rehearsal. We'll all meet up at the church after lunch so the vicar can tell us what we have to do and where we have to stand for the wedding.'

'When will we meet Rupert, Mary?' enquired Michael.

'He will see us at the church when he has finished his rounds.'

Lunch over, and Uncle Bertram sat himself down, hoping for a rest after eating rather too much.

'Oh, no you don't!' said Aunt Annie. 'There's no time for afternoon naps!'

'Well, that was some meal!' he exclaimed.

'Yes, I was hoping to join you too, Uncle Bertram! I could do with a sit-down for a little while!' declared Michael.

'It's only a short way to the church,' said Mary. 'The walk will do us all good.'

Michael groaned.

'Did you say something, Michael?' Lucy asked.

'Oh, – no.'

'I don't think it's good for the digestion, going for walks after a big meal!' proclaimed Uncle Bertram.

'Get away with you!' replied Aunt Annie. 'Once you sit down after lunch, you are there for at least an hour or more, and we have to be at the church to meet the vicar.'

Michael looked at Uncle Bertram to see if he was thinking the same as he was and when Uncle Bertram caught Michael's eye, a broad grin appeared on his face.

'Now,' said Aunt Annie, 'up you get -it's time we were on our way!'

Reluctantly, the two men followed her out of the door.

When they all arrived at the church, the vicar was already there to greet them and it wasn't long before Rupert appeared with his young brother, who was only six years old and who, when he saw Anthony, went straight over and sat down beside him.

While the vicar was talking to the grown-ups, the two boys slipped out of their pew and disappeared, so when it came to rehearsing walking up the aisle, the pair of them were nowhere to be seen! Thinking they might have gone outside to play, Michael went out of the church to look for them, but to no avail. Seeing the door to the belfry had been left open by the bell-ringers who had been practising earlier, he thought the boys might have tried to climb up to the bells, but again, they were not there. Lucy began to get worried, so Uncle Bertram tried to reassure her, saying that they must be somewhere inside the building.

After a thorough investigation, Rupert found them playing hide and seek in the vestry amongst the cassocks. Both boys were given a good ticking off for misbehaving – especially in a place of worship – and once they had rehearsed their part in the service without mishap, the family were able to make their way back to the farmhouse.

Uncle Bertram said to Mary, 'Take this, and get those two scallywags an ice-cream each!'

Michael laughed, 'You will be their friend for life now – Anthony loves ice-cream!'

William said, 'Michael, Rupert has invited us both to his Stag Night at 'The Cat and Fiddle tonight'. Shall we go for an hour or so? You're staying there anyway aren't you?'

'All right,' replied Michael. 'We can walk up together with Lucy and Anthony when it's time for Anthony to go to bed.'

'I doubt if he or anyone will get much sleep until after midnight, knowing what goes on at 'The Cat and Fiddle' – especially when there's a party on!' remarked Uncle Bertram with a chuckle.

'Oh, I don't think it's as bad as that,' said Mary.

'You obviously haven't heard what I've been told!' interrupted Peter, who had just come in from the farm.

'It sounds as if we're in for a noisy time tonight,' said Lucy, 'but I don't mind, just as long as we can get Anthony off to sleep!'

After they had finished supper, which lasted longer than usual, Uncle Bertram said, 'Have you got everything ready for tomorrow, Mary?'

'Yes, of course, Father. Mother and Caroline have made sure of that. My case is packed already! I only hope Rupert doesn't get too tipsy tonight, else I will have to prop him up as we walk back down the aisle tomorrow!' she laughed.

'You will have to keep an eye on him, Michael, and see he doesn't have too much to drink!' said Lucy.

Peter said, 'Once the party gets going, there's no telling what will happen. Rupert is known all over the village, and I expect they will all want to buy him a drink!'

'Oh, don't say that!' gasped Mary.

'I expect Harry will get him sobered up enough to be able to stand for the wedding,' laughed Uncle Bertram.

'That's enough of that sort of talk!' said Aunt Annie. 'I'm sure Rupert will be absolutely fine when the time comes.'

CHAPTER 36

As the evening advanced, Lucy said, 'Michael, I think we should be making a move so I can get Anthony to bed. He's starting to look very sleepy.'

Saying their farewells, Michael, William, Lucy and Anthony made their way to 'The Cat and Fiddle'.

When they arrived, the party was in full swing and a group of village lads were standing around the piano, finding voices they hadn't known they had and singing away, having the time of their lives!

Lucy quickly ushered Anthony up to their room, and shutting the door, said, 'After I have given you a wash, I will get you into bed and read you a story. Will you like that, Anthony?'

'Yes, please, Mummy,' he yawned.

Once he was in bed, Lucy opened the book, and it wasn't long before Anthony was fast asleep – in spite of the racket going on downstairs!

It was about eleven o'clock when Michael said goodnight to William and made his way up to join Lucy and Anthony.

'Don't make a noise!' Lucy whispered, 'He's asleep! Has William gone back to the farm?'

'Yes,' said Michael. 'I thought perhaps you might be asleep too when I came up.'

'What – with that noise going on? -Just listen! If I've heard that song once, I've heard it a dozen times. That's all they seem to know!'

'Which one's that?' teased Michael.

'It was a song about a man with a wooden leg!'

'Oh,' said Michael, starting to sing… 'Old Joe Furlong had a wooden leg…'

'Shh! You'll wake Anthony up! It sounded rather rude as time went on. Just listen to them now… I thought public houses closed at ten thirty!'

'They do normally, but the landlord managed to get an extension for tonight – until midnight.'

Lucy groaned, 'So I don't expect we'll get much sleep until then! That pianist must have incredible stamina to keep playing for so long!'

'They keep putting drinks on the piano for her. By the time it's midnight, someone will have to carry her home if she gets through that lot!' laughed Michael.

It wasn't long before he was fast asleep. Only Lucy was wide awake, and it wasn't until much later that she finally settled down for the night.

The day of the wedding started off with a cloudy sky. Needless to say, there wasn't much doing in 'The Cat and Fiddle' until nine o'clock that morning, when the family went down for breakfast. Afterwards, Michael, Lucy and Anthony went for a walk in the village, finishing up at the farmhouse just as the sun came out. William was sitting on the sofa, looking a little worse for wear after the previous night's party. Michael said, 'I wonder how Rupert is this morning? I hope he got home all right last night! – We will know he did if he manages to turn up at two o'clock this afternoon for his wedding!'

'I wonder how many of the lads will have spent the night on the village green?' said William. 'Some of them had already had too much to drink when we came away and would have had to sleep it off before going home!'

'Michael, I think it's time we returned to 'The Cat and Fiddle' to get ready now,' said Lucy.

'We'll see you all at the church,' added Michael. 'Come on, Anthony!'

The little church had been beautifully decorated and looked a picture with the sun shining through the windows. It seemed the whole village had turned out for the occasion.

Michael and William were relieved to see Rupert arrive, striding purposefully with his best man to their places in the front pew, followed shortly afterwards by Mary, on the arm of her father. As they walked up the aisle, Uncle Bertram turned and winked mischievously at Michael, who duly reciprocated, grinning broadly!

The wedding went off without any mishaps on the part of the two page boys, who had great fun throwing confetti at Mary and Rupert when the service was over!

The reception was held in the village hall and at the end of the meal, after the bridegroom and best man had spoken, Uncle Bertram got up and gave a very witty speech which made everyone laugh, especially when he referred to the previous evening's goings-on at 'The Cat and Fiddle', and the after-effects experienced by some of the participants who ended up spending a rather uncomfortable night on the village green! He concluded by wishing his daughter, Mary, and her husband, all the happiness in the world.

Once the applause had died down, bride and groom circulated amongst their guests until they slipped away to get changed at the farmhouse. With their suitcases already packed, they returned briefly to say goodbye, before leaving for their honeymoon.

'William, are you coming to 'The Cat and Fiddle' tonight?' Michael asked.

'I don't think so,' replied William. 'Caroline thought it would be nice to spend the evening with Uncle Bertram and Aunt Annie as they are bound to miss Mary. Why don't you and Lucy come for a short while? It will be quieter there than at the public house.'

'I'll ask Lucy, I'm sure she will say yes, she didn't approve of some of the things she heard last night! -By the way, what time are you going home tomorrow, William?'

'We'll be catching the ten thirty train.'

'That's the one we'll be on!' said Michael. 'We can all travel together!'

After Michael had spoken to Lucy, they all made their way back to the farmhouse to join Uncle Bertram and family for a celebratory drink.

'It will seem very strange not having Mary around,' said Aunt Annie. 'I shall miss her nipping about in the kitchen, helping me with the meals…'

'I shouldn't get too upset, Mother,' said Uncle Bertram, 'she'll still be in the village and I'm sure Mary will often come to see us, won't she, Caroline?'

'Of course she will!'

'Why don't we have a singsong?' suggested Peter.

'That's a good idea,' said William, and for the next hour they sang happily through all the old favourites until it was time for Anthony to go to bed, when Michael and

Lucy said their farewells, and the three of them left for 'The Cat and Fiddle.'

As they drew near the public house, Michael said, 'I can hear them singing again!' Then he started.. 'Underneath the lamplight, by the…'

'That's enough of that!' remarked Lucy, 'We will have enough trouble getting this young man off to sleep without you adding to the problem.'

As they climbed the stairs to their room, Lucy said, 'I don't expect we'll get to sleep until it's closing time although Anthony actually seems to be enjoying the singing from downstairs – as long as they keep off the song about the man with the wooden leg… I don't want him picking up any more bad words, he knows too many already from his visits to the farm!'

The next morning, after saying their farewells to the landlord and his wife, they made their way to the railway station to join William and Caroline for the journey home.

'What time did you manage to get off to sleep last night?' enquired William.

'I should think it was about half an hour after closing time,' said Michael. 'I must say they seem to enjoy life here in Wentley village!'

'I know!' said Lucy, 'but some of the songs are rather vulgar.'

William laughed, 'The night before, they had to stand either side of the pianist to stop her falling off the piano stool because they were buying her drinks all evening.'

'Shh!' said Lucy. 'Little ears!'

Anthony, who up till then had remained silent, suddenly said, 'Mummy, what did happen to the man with the wooden leg?'

Epilogue

When Lord Barnes returned from his stay in London, he wanted to hear all about Mary's wedding and how Anthony had carried out his page boy duties. After William had finished telling him, Michael couldn't resist adding a colourful account of the lively time they had experienced at 'The Cat and Fiddle'!

Lord Barnes then reported that the Police Inspector had been to see him with the news that Felix had been sent back to prison, although the other man was still at large.

'I wonder if everything's all right in the Druly household now?' asked William.

'It is, as far as I know,' replied his father. 'I think Joe realises how fortunate he is to be alive and able to enjoy being with his family. I may not have told you that he came to see me a while back asking how to contact Matt Schulz because he wanted to thank him for saving his life, and of course, I was only too pleased to be of help.

I do hope things will now return to normal, and that we can all get on with running the Estate.'

Postscript

One morning, a few weeks later, a letter arrived addressed to Mr Joe Druly, and this is what it said:

Dear Mr Druly,

Thank you for writing to me.

I hope by now your wounds have healed.

I am pleased that you and Betty are together again after our two nations' bitter struggle. Now that is over, perhaps we can all live peacefully and put the horrors of war behind us.

I have been fortunate to meet up with a childhood sweetheart and we hope to marry in the not too distant future.

Best wishes,
Matt Schulz.

The End

About the Author

Stanley Scott was brought up in the fenland of East Anglia and was a chorister at Ely Cathedral. After returning from service in the Royal Navy in 1946, he worked as an electrician until accepting the post of Senior Electrician at Grafham Water in 1966, later becoming Electrical Superintendent. He remained there until his retirement twenty five years later.

From then on he spent most of his time engaged in DIY and six years ago became interested in model trains.

He began writing in 2019 and now at the age of 96, has just completed this, his second book.

Thank You

I am enormously grateful to those of my friends who have encouraged and assisted me in the preparation of this story, especially Anne, Geoff and Liz.

Thank you to my younger daughter, Adrienne, and to my granddaughter, Alicia, and her husband, Mark, for their support and input, and to my grandson, Joshua, who introduced me to the small book mentioned in the story. He obtained a replica edition of an 'Active Service' Saint John's Gospel, which was originally produced during the First World War by the Scripture Gift Mission. Copies were issued to soldiers and were the perfect size to fit into the front pocket of their uniforms. Each little book had a message printed inside from the war hero, Lord Roberts.

Special thanks go to my daughter Vanessa, without whom this book would not have reached publication, and to our friend, Terry Barringer, for help with editing.